Abby, Tried and True

Also by Donna Gephart

The Paris Project

In Your Shoes

Lily and Dunkin

Death by Toilet Paper

How to Survive Middle School

Olivia Bean, Trivia Queen

*As If Being 12¾ Isn't Bad Enough,
My Mother Is Running for President!*

Abby, Tried and True

DONNA GEPHART

Simon & Schuster Books for Young Readers

New York   London   Toronto   Sydney   New Delhi

SIMON & SCHUSTER BOOKS FOR YOUNG READERS
An imprint of Simon & Schuster Children's Publishing Division
1230 Avenue of the Americas, New York, New York 10020

SIMON & SCHUSTER BOOKS FOR YOUNG READERS
is a trademark of Simon & Schuster, Inc.
For information about special discounts for bulk purchases,
please contact Simon & Schuster Special Sales
at 1-866-506-1949 or business@simonandschuster.com.
The Simon & Schuster Speakers Bureau can bring authors to your live event.
For more information or to book an event, contact the Simon & Schuster Speakers
Bureau at 1-866-248-3049 or visit our website at www.simonspeakers.com.
Jacket design by Chloë Foglia
Interior design by Tom Daly
The text for this book was set in Adobe Garamond Pro.
Manufactured in the United States of America
0121 FFG
First Edition
2 4 6 8 10 9 7 5 3 1
Library of Congress Cataloging-in-Publication Data
Names: Gephart, Donna, author.
Title: Abby, tried and true / Donna Gephart.
Description: First edition. | New York City : Simon & Schuster Books for
Young Readers, [2020] | Audience: Ages 8–12. | Audience: Grades 4–6. | Summary:
Abby Braverman strives to navigate seventh grade without her best friend, keep up
her older brother's spirits while he undergoes cancer treatment, and figure out her
surprising new feelings for the boy next door. Includes facts about testicular cancer.
Identifiers: LCCN 2020002284 (print) | ISBN 9781534440890 (hardcover)
| ISBN 9781534440913 (eBook)
Subjects: CYAC: Change—Fiction. | Cancer—Fiction. | Brothers and sisters—
Fiction. | Middle schools—Fiction. | Schools—Fiction. | Lesbian mothers—Fiction.
Classification: LCC PZ7.G293463 Abb 2020 (print) | DDC [Fic]—dc23
LC record available at https://lccn.loc.gov/2020002284

Dedicated to my amazing agent, Tina Dubois. I can barely believe
my great good fortune that Tina has been my literary agent, my friend, my
dispenser of wisdom, editorial feedback, and support, shepherding my eight
novels and one picture book into the world since we began working together
in 2005. Here's to many more creative literary adventures together!
Go, team!

"You can never get a cup of tea large enough
or a book long enough to suit me."
—C. S. Lewis

Abby Braverman thought the worst thing that could happen was her best (and only) friend, Catriella Wasserman, moving 6,584.2 miles away from her home next door to Abby in Port Paradise, Florida, to Jerusalem, Israel, the summer Abby turned twelve.

She was wrong.

The Almost-Worst Day

Gnawing at her thumbnail while standing in the driveway and gushing sweat like an open fire hydrant, Abby watched her moms—Mom Rachel with her puffy ponytail and Mama Dee with her short, dark hair—hug Ms. Wasserman for all she was worth, while an airport shuttle van idled nearby in the street.

The three women separated, wiping away tears, even though they were the strongest women Abby knew.

Cat, with her silky, straight brown hair, rushed over and clutched Abby, her warm tears mingling with Abby's and Abby's with hers on both of their cheeks. Abby was memorizing how Cat felt—bony and warm; how she smelled—mango shampoo and lavender soap; and how she sounded—sniffly and sad.

"Come on now, you two," Mama Dee said.

Ms. Wasserman sighed. "The van driver is waiting, Catriella."

"Give them another minute," Mom Rachel murmured.

Eventually, the moms needed to grab the girls' shoulders to pry them apart, like separating tangled roots of garden plants, and guide them away from each other.

"Don't leave," Abby whispered. It felt like a part of herself was going—the best part.

Cat shook her head. "I wish—"

The van driver honked.

Suddenly, Cat wriggled from her mom's grip and ran back to Abby. She handed her a rectangular package. "Got this for you."

"But I didn't get you anything."

"I don't need anything." Cat put up a hand to wave or surrender.

Abby wasn't sure which.

Then Cat and her mom boarded the van, which drove down the street and was gone.

Mom Rachel held on to Abby. Mama Dee held on to Mom Rachel. The three of them clung to one another like crumbling pillars, barely able to support each other.

Long after her moms clasped each other's hands and went inside, Abby stood in the driveway, sweat stinging her eyes, and stared at the avocado-green house next door. The one with the red door she'd gone through hundreds of times to have dinners and sleepovers, listen to Cat practice violin, read books, bake cookies, and recently, gossip about the boys Cat liked.

Cat and her mom didn't live in that house anymore.

It seemed impossible that Cat wouldn't be bursting through the door to share a bit of news with Abby or join her when she walked Miss Lucy to the neighborhood park around the corner.

Abby wondered if she or Cat ached more over the move and decided it was harder for the person being left behind because the other person at least had exciting new adventures ahead.

"Don't you dare forget about me, Catriella Robyn Wasserman," she whispered fiercely to no one before going inside.

In Abby's bedroom with the blue-and-green afghan her Bubbe Marcia had crocheted for her on the bed; her bookshelf filled with books about turtles, fantasy novels, and poetry collections from the bookstore in town; and the tank of her red-eared slider turtle, Fudge, on her desk, Abby sat on her bed and unwrapped the gift Cat had given her. She ran her fingers over the image of a forest path on the hardback journal's cover and read the quote.

> What is it you plan to do with your one
> wild and precious life? —Mary Oliver

"Good question, Mary Oliver," Abby said to the dead poet.

Of course Cat had found a journal with the last line from her favorite poem—"The Summer Day." Abby would use the journal for important things, like writing poems and thoughts she wanted to share with Cat.

Abby opened to the first page and poured her pain into a poem, her pen making satisfying black scars on the cream-colored surface.

Going . . .
(a poem for two voices, one of whom isn't here)

Away.
Please stay.
Toward Israel.
Please . . .
So far, far away . . .
Stay.
From here.

A New Wild
and Precious Day

After sleeping for fourteen hours, Abby woke to the smell of French toast, which made zero sense. Mama Dee would be at her bakery shop in town—Dee's Delights—creating specialty cupcakes and birthday cake masterpieces for her customers. Mom Rachel was probably still asleep because she stayed up late some nights editing videos for her YouTube channel, *Lettuce Eat*. Also, anything Mom Rachel created in the kitchen smelled savory, not sweet. Abby's brother, Paul, who was sixteen, usually slept till noon—it was summer break, after all. Miss Lucy, their princess-y dachshund dog with the world's stubbiest legs, couldn't reach the griddle without a catapult. And Abby's turtle, Fudge, was in his tank on a rock, sunning himself under the heat lamp.

Abby wondered if it was worth getting her heavy heart out of bed to solve the French toast mystery. She ran a hand through her long, knotty hair, and her fingers got stuck. She knew she should brush it, but she didn't have the energy.

Against her better judgment, Abby found herself shuffling barefoot toward the kitchen.

Bluegrass music played through the speakers in the sunny kitchen.

Paul wore Mom Rachel's COOKING IS MY SUPERPOWER apron. His thick, dark hair was wide awake, sticking up in forty-two divergent directions.

"Paul?"

Her brother, spatula in hand, turned. "Hey there, Six-Pack!"

His nickname for Abby came from the shortened version—"Abs"—that Paul turned into "Six-Pack."

"Hey," Abby replied with all the energy of a dying houseplant.

Miss Lucy waddled over, her long ears flopping and the tags on her collar jangling. She didn't care that Abby's heart was shattered. She had needs. Miss Lucy, in her fake diamond–studded collar with her dachshund princess attitude, always had needs.

When Abby bent to pet her, Miss Lucy sneezed twice on her hand, then returned to her spot near Paul.

"Love you too," Abby muttered.

"These bad boys are almost done." Paul flipped each of the slices. The French toast sizzled, smelling like warm butter. "How many slices?" Paul tossed one piece so high, it somersaulted before landing back on the griddle. "Booyah! Thought you might flip for my French toast, Six-Pack."

"Not funny," Abby said.

"Absolutely funny." Paul did a dramatic turn and added a few shakes of Penzeys cinnamon to all the slices. "It's going to be so good."

Abby scowled at Paul for being happy the day after Cat left. "Half a slice, please."

"Two thick slices with warm syrup coming up."

Abby rested her chin on her hands. "I love warm syrup."

"I know."

Abby remembered how Cat would drown her French toast in a river of syrup. Something squeezed her chest so tightly, she almost said *ouch*. "Paul?"

"Yeah?"

"Nothing."

"It'll get better, Six-Pack."

It took everything Abby had not to burst into tears because she knew Paul was wrong and she'd feel this way forever. "It won't get better," Abby mumbled.

"It will." Paul put a plate in front of Abby. It had two slices of thick French toast with powdered sugar sprinkled on top, syrup drizzled over that, and a few raspberries and a couple mint leaves on the side. "I know it seems impossible right now without Cat, but time will make it better."

Abby tried to smile to show Paul she appreciated his efforts to make her feel better, but the muscles around her mouth were apparently on strike. She pushed words past the gravel in her throat. "This looks good, Paul. You take after Mom."

"Which one?"

That was their perpetual joke. In their two-mom family, both were magicians in the kitchen—Mom Rachel with savory dishes and Mama Dee with baked goods. They'd met when they worked at the same fancy-pants restaurant in the city, Philomela's, but that was a long time ago, before they embarked on their own business ventures.

Paul placed his plate on the counter with *four!* slices of French toast.

The moms' bedroom door opened.

Mom Rachel came out wearing her usual attire—overalls and a purple T-shirt; a scarf tying back her curly black hair, which was up in a ponytail; and rainbow high-top sneakers.

"Morning." She kissed Abby on the head, then walked over to the griddle and sniffed. "Mmm."

Paul reached for another plate. "Want some? I made plenty."

"I'll have some later. Thanks, honey." Mom Rachel bent and petted Miss Lucy. "How's my best girl doing?"

Miss Lucy whipped her thin tail side to side.

If Abby had a tail, it would be droopy, and no amount of petting would perk it up.

Mom Rachel grabbed some canvas bags. "I'm going to the food co-op to pick up things for a new *Lettuce Eat* video I'm making later today."

Paul took off the apron. "Maybe I can help."

"That would be great." Mom popped a raspberry into her mouth. "Maybe you can help too, Abs."

Abby raised her eyebrows. She never helped her mom film videos for *Lettuce Eat*. There was no way Abby would get in

front of a camera for the whole world to see. She knew she'd
feel like a turtle with its shell ripped off. But that didn't stop
her mom from asking her.

Paul climbed onto the stool next to Abby and dug into
his breakfast. "What're you doing today? Besides feeling
miserable?"

Abby stabbed a raspberry and shrugged. She didn't like
thinking about summer days without Cat here with her.

Paul got up, went into the garage, and returned with their
Monopoly game. "Was hoping you'd have time for me to
kick your butt."

"Sorry. I'll have to kick *your* butt another day."

"Hey!" Paul batted his long eyelashes at her. "I'll let you
have the dog token."

The dog token was Abby's favorite, but she wished they
had a turtle token she could move around the board extra
slowly. "It's just—"

"You can be banker, too."

"You've made it impossible to refuse you."

"I know." Paul bumped his shoulder into hers.

Abby finished her French toast. Every delicious bite.

Because even sad people needed to eat.

After Abby trounced Paul at Monopoly by buying all the
railroads, as well as the orange, yellow, and green properties, and then building hotels on them, she retreated
to her bedroom without even her signature Monopoly-
winning victory dance, which included a few deep bows,

fist pumps, and an assortment of whoops and hollers.

"Hi, Fudge," Abby said to her turtle, who was swimming in his tank, oblivious to Abby's anguish.

She settled onto her bed, sitting up against the headboard with the blue-and-green afghan—which looked like the pattern of a turtle's shell—spread over her lap. Abby was determined to stay in bed until, oh, the start of seventh grade.

Then she decided to do something that usually made her feel better. She reached under her bed and pulled out her endless afghan. Bubbe Marcia had taught Abby how to crochet, and Abby got the idea of creating an afghan with no end. When Abby ran out of yarn, she just started with a new skein in a different color. "I can't wait to show Bubbe Marcia how big it's grown since last time she was here," Abby said to Fudge, who was clearly ignoring her.

While crocheting, Abby heard the front door open and a voice call out, "Yo, Paul. Ready?"

It was Paul's buddy Jake, who Abby imagined wearing a tank top and flexing his biceps because he often wore a tank top and flexed his biceps.

"Let's go!" Paul's friend Ethan yelled.

"The three Musketeers together again," Abby grumbled. She turned to Fudge. "It's not fair that Paul has two good friends who live nearby and I have zero." The thought made her stomach hurt.

"Be right there," Paul called from his room, which was directly across the hall from Abby's.

"Grabbing food," Jake said.

"Me too," Ethan added.

There was a knock on Abby's door, which made her grip her endless afghan more tightly, the crochet hook biting into the crook of her hand. "Yeah?" she asked timidly.

Her door flung open, and Paul marched in, followed by Jake and Ethan, who were stuffing their faces with French toast. No warm maple syrup. No berries and mint leaves on the side. No plates.

At this point, only Abby's eyes and forehead showed above her protective endless afghan shield.

"Let's go, Six-Pack." Paul tugged on the afghan.

"Huh?" Abby lowered it a few inches, like a turtle tentatively poking its head from its shell.

Ethan leaped onto the bottom of Abby's bed, making it creak. "Yeah, let's go."

Abby was sure her bed would crash to the floor, but it held steady. "Where?"

"We're taking you to the movies," Paul said.

"Me?" Paul never let Abby join when he and his friends went out anywhere.

"Who else, dingbat?" Ethan asked.

Jake was busy flexing his muscles in front of Abby's full-length mirror.

Paul grabbed the pillow from behind Abby's head and threw it at Jake.

"Hey!" Jake yelled.

"You're going to break my sister's mirror with your ugly face."

Jake threw the pillow back at Paul. "You're going to break it with this, moron."

"It's a pillow," Paul said. "It couldn't break wind."

Ethan cracked up and fell over on the bed.

Paul gave a little bow.

Abby touched her hair, which was a little greasy. "I need a shower."

Paul waved his hand in front of his nose. "You do!"

Ethan stood and popped Paul in the chest with the back of his hand. "Don't be mean to the Abster."

"Ouch." Paul hunched forward. "Don't do that again."

"I didn't even hit you hard."

"It hurt." Paul punched Ethan in the shoulder.

"Stop!" Abby yelled. "I need to get ready."

The boys filed out of her room, shoving one another and laughing.

Once they were in the hallway, Abby put her endless afghan back under her bed. "Going to the movies will be way more fun than crocheting," she whispered to Fudge.

"Hurry," Paul called. "Don't want to miss the previews."

Abby grabbed jeans and a long-sleeved T-shirt because even though it was hot outside, it would be cold in the theater. "I know you love the previews. I'm hurrying!"

In the chilly theater between Ethan and Paul with Jake on the far end, Abby sat tall. She munched on the popcorn Paul had bought her and lost herself in the horror movie, startling every few minutes to the delight of the guys and completely forgetting to be miserable about missing Cat.

When they got home, the house smelled like frying onions, garlic, and dill. It reminded Abby of their family Rosh Hashanah and Passover dinners, when Mom Rachel made mouthwateringly delicious matzo ball soup.

"Hey, Mom," Paul called.

"You're home," Mom Rachel said.

Abby got to the kitchen first.

"Butterbean! Just in time to help with my cooking video." She handed Abby an apron.

Abby scooted past. "Um, no thanks!"

Paul grabbed the apron. "I've got this."

"Good. I always get more views when you're in the videos, Paul."

"That's because of my irresistible charm and good looks."

Mom Rachel flicked Paul's earlobe. "I think it's your sense of humor."

"That, too," Paul said. "And my modesty. People love how incredibly funny, suave, and modest I am."

Mom shook her head at Paul, but Abby could tell she loved his goofing around.

Abby wished she had the courage to stand in front of the camera like Paul. She'd be more comfortable if she could feel like she was speaking to one person, but being on camera felt like she'd be talking to thousands of people, which was overwhelming.

But Paul loved it. Once, he jumped around the house like he'd won the lottery when Cooking4Five wrote in the comments of one of Mom's videos, "Paul should be a stand-up comic. He's hilarious!"

Abby went into her bedroom and kept the door open so she could listen to them making the video. In their small one-story house, it was easy to hear everything going on if she left the door open.

"You might want to add a splash of wine to the pan," Mom Rachel said.

Paul added, "Or you might want to add a splash of wine to your glass. Cheers!"

Abby pictured Paul toasting with an imaginary glass. People watching would laugh at that part. Why couldn't Abby be relaxed like him and help make Mom's cooking videos? Abby told herself nobody wanted to watch a quiet turtle cook a meal. Nobody.

Abby watched Fudge swim around his tank. "Mom will be on her own with videos in a couple days," she told Fudge. "Paul's leaving for Camp Shalom. He's going to be a counselor-in-training this year."

Fudge ignored Abby and kept swimming, as turtles do.

"It's good for Paul because he loves that camp, but bad for me. What am I supposed to do with both Cat and Paul gone?"

Fudge didn't have an answer for that one.

Something caught Abby's eye.

Not something, but some*one*.

Abby pushed up the slats of her window blinds and gasped.

A car with a U-Haul trailer attached had pulled into the driveway next door—Cat's driveway!—and two people got out of the car.

Abby pulled the blinds out of the way entirely and pressed her cheek to the warm window.

One of the people was a woman with a blond ponytail, shorts, a T-shirt, and running shoes. She looked about her moms' age, maybe a little younger.

The other person walking toward Cat's house was a boy about Abby's age, with light brown hair falling over one eye. He was wearing a tank top, jean shorts, and flip-flops.

A fierce, blinding anger caught Abby off guard. How dare anyone move into Cat's house! She stood back, giving her heartbeat a chance to slow. Abby knew she shouldn't feel betrayed because Ms. Wasserman had told her moms she'd planned to rent out their home in case they decided to come back early.

Abby crossed her fingers, hoping they would.

"Don't even bother moving all your junk in," Abby said. "The Wassermans will probably be coming home soon." But Ms. Wasserman was so excited about her new job at the Hebrew University of Jerusalem, Abby knew they wouldn't be coming home early.

She peeked through the blinds again.

The boy carried a laundry basket overflowing with clothes into the house. His biceps were flexed, which reminded Abby of Paul's friend Jake, always making muscles.

Abby wanted to run out and tell her mom and brother,

but they were in the middle of making a video, and she didn't dare interrupt. Instead, Abby grabbed her phone. She thought she'd take a photo of the new boy and send it to Cat, then realized doing that would be creepy and an invasion of his privacy. She wouldn't want someone taking her photo when she didn't know about it. But Abby could still tell Cat about him, so it would be almost like she was there.

Abby started to call Cat, but then she remembered it was seven hours later in Israel. Cat would already be asleep. So she pulled out the journal and wrote a description of the new boy so she could share it later with Cat.

> Hair over one eye makes him look mysterious.
> Carrying things makes him look strong.
> No books or pets makes him look like someone
> I won't like. ☹
> Come back, Cat!

"And that," Abby heard Mom Rachel say from the kitchen, "is that. Recipe in the description below and in our e-cookbook, which is available for purchase. Please subscribe to our channel, like this video, and share it with your friends."

"Or your enemies!" Paul shouted. "Everybody's got to eat. Am I right?"

"Right. We'll see you next week at *Lettuce Eat* when we make another awesome vegetarian recipe together," Mom Rachel said. "Peace and good eats."

Abby sank onto her bed and hugged her pillow to her chest. *The new people next door are my enemies*, she thought. *I don't care if they eat.*

Mom Rachel and Paul laughed in the kitchen.

Their laughter felt like sandpaper on Abby's brain.

Fudge sunned himself on a rock under the heat lamp as though he were on vacation.

"How am I supposed to get through the rest of summer by myself with other people living next door in Cat's house?"

As usual, Fudge had zero words of wisdom to offer.

Good-Byes Are the Pits

The drive to drop Paul off at the camp bus went too quickly. Abby wasn't ready to let him go yet, even though she didn't say a word to him during the ride and mostly stared out the window as they whooshed past palm trees, office buildings, and strip malls.

"Camp in Florida is weird," Mom Rachel said. "It ends a few days before school starts."

"Tell me about it," Paul said. "I'll hardly have any time to get ready for school. And I'm always exhausted after camp ends. Seems like school starts earlier and earlier every year."

"It really does." Mom tapped a beat on the steering wheel in rhythm with the Lizzo song coming from the radio. "If you lived in Pennsylvania, where our friends June and Caren and their daughter, Monica, live, you'd still have three weeks of summer after camp ended."

"Or in Israel," Abby muttered. "They start in September too."

No one responded.

In the parking lot, Paul had already hoisted his huge duffel bag from the trunk and hugged Mom by the time Abby dragged herself from the back seat of the car.

She was tired of good-byes. Abby leaned against the hot car, crossed her arms, and nodded toward Paul.

"What's that about, Six-Pack?" Paul dropped his duffel with a thud, ran over, grabbed Abby around the waist, and swung her around. "Houston, we have liftoff!"

"Paul!"

He put her down, held a hand to his lower back, and winced.

"You okay, sweetheart?" Mom Rachel walked toward him.

He waved her concern away. "Look, Abs," Paul said. "I'll be back before you know it, and you'd better have Monopoly set up because I'm going to get revenge on you for crushing me the other day."

Abby smiled but refused to uncross her arms.

Then she did uncross them because she needed her arms open to give her brother a bone-crunching hug that would have to last her the three weeks he was gone. "Love you, Paul."

Paul squeezed back. "Love you too. Be good."

Abby wondered what else she could be.

Then she watched her brother walk across the parking lot toward the camp bus, where families milled around like ants circling a spot of jam left on a countertop.

Paul pivoted and yelled, "And don't touch my banjo, Abigail Braverman! I'll know!"

She cupped her hands around her mouth. "I won't!"

They both knew she probably would. Abby loved putting on the three steel finger picks and pretending she was a famous banjo player onstage, even though her audience at home consisted of Fudge and sometimes Miss Lucy.

Mom Rachel held one hand over her eyes, either to shield them from the sun or to hide the fact that she might cry, and held the other hand up to wave to Paul, even though he wasn't looking at either of them.

Abby chewed a thumbnail as she watched Paul throw his duffel bag underneath the bus in the storage area, say hi to some friends, and climb onto the bus.

The bus roared away with her brother on it.

Abby had to squint extra hard to keep tears from leaking out. She didn't want to cry in front of Mom Rachel and hear again about how sensitive she was being. Abby reminded herself that Paul would be only 126 miles away, and he'd be home in three weeks. Still, those tears fought to escape. She sniffed hard to keep them bottled up.

"Come on, baby girl." Mom Rachel slung an arm over Abby's shoulders. "We're going to Daniel's Diner to cheer ourselves up. Good-byes are the pits."

Abby loved Daniel's Diner. Their potatoes au gratin was her favorite side dish to go with the bean-and-beet burger, along with pickle spears and spicy coleslaw. Mom Rachel usually chose a big salad with a glass of fresh-pressed juice. Cat used to order loaded tater tots, minus the bacon, with hot sauce on the side; she always came with Abby and Mom Rachel to drop Paul off and go to the diner afterward.

This would be Mom Rachel and Abby's first year going to Daniel's Diner without Cat.

On the drive home, Abby somehow managed to feel stuffed and empty at the same time. She'd ordered loaded tater tots this time—no hot sauce or bacon—and could understand why Cat loved them.

Before Mom Rachel pulled into their driveway, Abby saw him.

The new boy.

He was mowing the Wassermans' lawn, and he wasn't wearing a shirt.

"I guess we'll have to go over and say hello to the new people." Mom Rachel sighed.

Abby nodded, but her hands were fists because she wasn't ready to meet the new people. She was still angry they'd moved into Cat's house. "I'm not up to it right now."

"Neither am I." Mom Rachel squeezed the steering wheel. "I still think Miriam's going to walk out that door and come over to chat. It's hard to imagine her so far away."

"It's 6,584.2 miles," Abby muttered.

"Huh?"

"Nothing." Abby hadn't considered how much her mom might be missing her friend Miriam—Ms. Wasserman. This had to be hard on both of her moms. Abby should have been more thoughtful. She wasn't the only person who lost a friend when the Wassermans moved to Israel.

Inside, Mom Rachel stood in the foyer and sighed.

"When Paul's not here, it's so . . . quiet." She looked at Abby. "I don't like it."

As if to prove her wrong, Miss Lucy came running, dog tags jangling.

Mom Rachel scooped Miss Lucy into her arms and nuzzled her. "Who's my best wittle girl?"

Abby shuffled through the house to her room. She glanced behind her at Paul's door and considered going in and playing his banjo just because he said not to, but instead she pushed open the door to her own room and walked over to Fudge's tank.

Abby was sure her mom's comment about the quiet house was intended for her. *She* was too quiet. *She* wasn't as social as Paul. *She* wasn't as much fun to have around the house.

Abby pressed her fingertips against the tank. "It's not easy being a turtle. Is it, Fudge?"

He swam toward her fingertips.

It made Abby smile. "You're the best little—"

The sound of a lawn mower cut through Abby's words. She opened her blinds. New Boy was sweating and struggling to push the mower through thick Saint Augustine grass. The Wassermans used to hire someone to cut the grass, but he hadn't been there in a while.

Abby wondered what kind of person New Boy was. Did he like playing sports? Reading? Cooking? Dancing? Singing? Was he loud and funny? Quiet and serious? Was he the kind of boy who might like to play Monopoly with his next-door neighbor?

Because, for an interloper, he was cute and looked like he might be nice.

Too bad Abby would probably never speak to him, especially without Cat nearby to lend her courage. Cat always knew the right words to say and how to make people laugh and feel comfortable. Abby was especially good at creating awkward silences.

She closed the blinds, sank down onto her bed, and watched Fudge quietly paddle through the water in his tank, getting nowhere.

Abby realized she could go out and check the mail. If she happened to say hello to New Boy, that wouldn't be the worst thing.

She brushed her hair and put clear gloss on her lips, then leashed up Miss Lucy and walked outside. Abby was too nervous to look over at New Boy and went directly to the mailbox across the street. On her way back, he looked at her and stopped pushing the mower. He turned it off and waved.

Abby waved back. "Hi!"

"Hey!" he said in a deep, friendly voice.

Before Abby could figure out what to say next, she stepped forward and promptly tripped over Miss Lucy, landing hard on her palms on the spiky grass. "Oomph!"

"Are you—"

Abby didn't hear another word New Boy said because she ran into the house and to her room, not even taking the leash off Miss Lucy.

"I knew I shouldn't have tried to talk to him," she told Fudge. "What was I thinking?"

Fudge looked at her through the glass of the tank with his mouth open.

"Stop looking at me in that tone of voice! I'm hopeless!" Fudge didn't argue.

Abby went into the living room to take off Miss Lucy's leash, then pulled out her phone to text Cat. It took about one second for her to decide that Cat didn't need to know what a fool she'd made of herself in front of New Boy. Instead, she got right to the important stuff.

> Miss you. We dropped Paul off for camp, and you weren't there to eat tater tots at the diner afterward, so I was forced to do it for you.

A few minutes later, Cat responded.

> Forced, huh? Did you put hot sauce on them?

Abby laughed.

> No! They were good, though. Just not as good without you there.

Cat replied right away.

> Sorry Paul's at camp and I'm not there. We'd have had so much fun going on adventures if I didn't have to move away. It's boring here without you. Love you, Abs.

Abby wiped tears with the back of her hand.

Love you too, Cat.

Then she put her phone away because texting Cat made
her sad.

She pulled out her journal, stared at the wall, listened to
the quiet in the house, and wrote a poem.

Stopping Time Can Be Dangerous

Sometimes, I wish
I had magic powers
And could stop time
At the best moment (me and Cat together)
And it would stay like that
Forever. . . .
But it would be awful
If time got stuck
At the worst moment (tripping in front of
New Boy)
And stayed like that
Forever. . . .
Maybe it's a good thing
Time keeps ticking on.
Happy-sad. Sad-happy.
Ticktock. Ticktock.

Abby 2.0 Has a Big Day

A week and a half later, Abby woke on her twelfth birthday to her phone ringing.

She tried to turn it off because she thought it was an alarm and it was time to get up for school. Then Abby remembered Paul was still at camp and school didn't start for another twelve days.

Squinting at the phone, Abby saw Cat's photo from when their families went on vacation together and Cat had nearly fallen out of her kayak. Abby pressed the button to video chat.

Cat's real-life image came into view, and Abby felt joy spread through her. "Hey!" Abby shouted. "Love your French braid."

Cat shook her head side to side, the brown braid whipping each way. "Mom did it for me. Got tired of wearing it straight or up in a ponytail."

"Looks very chic."

"Merci!" Cat struck a pose, and both girls laughed. "Hey,

Abs, I wanted to be the first to wish you a happy birthday."

Abby looked at the time—10:07 a.m. "You succeeded."

"Yes! Are you just waking up?"

Running fingers through her thick hair, Abby blinked a few times. "Uh, yeah. I look like donkey butt. Don't I?"

Cat threw her head back and laughed. It sounded like fireworks bursting in a night sky. "You definitely don't look like donkey butt. I'll prove it."

Suddenly, Abby was watching Ms. Wasserman cook at a stove.

"Mom, tell Abby she doesn't look like donkey butt."

"Language, Catriella!" Ms. Wasserman's nose took up the whole screen, then her right eyeball. "Happy birthday, Abigail. You look lovely, sweetheart."

The image quickly changed back to Cat. "Sheesh, Mom. Abby doesn't need to see your nose hairs up close and personal."

"Catriella!"

Cat laughed softly.

Abby leaned over to look at Fudge in his tank.

"Is that Fudge? Oh, let me see him."

Abby turned the screen so Cat could watch Fudge swim.

Cat squealed. "I miss that little guy."

"Yeah, he's a cutie."

"How's Miss Lucy doing?"

"Spoiled as ever."

Cat whispered, "I begged Mom for a dog. They have cool kinds of dogs here, and I figured she felt guilty enough for moving me away from you that she'd give in. But guess what she said?"

"'No'?"

Cat yelled, "She said no because she's cruel and unusual!"

"Knock it off, Catriella, or you can hang up. Dinner in five minutes."

"Sorry, Mom." But Cat winked to show Abby she wasn't really sorry.

"It's so weird you're about to have dinner and I just woke up," Abby said.

"No," Cat replied. "It's weird that you're waking up when it's dinnertime."

"Time is weird," Abby said, thinking of her poem.

"Lots of things are weird." Cat examined chipped polish on one of her fingernails. "So tell me about your birthday extravaganza plans. Same as usual?"

Abby rummaged through her drawers, looking for something to wear. "Same as usual, except you won't be here, which stinks."

"It does stink. We've never missed each other's birthdays."

"Never. Remember on your ninth birthday, your mom wanted to do something special, and she took us to that amusement park, and you went on the roller coaster something like six times in a row?"

"Nine times in a row," Cat corrected. "Because it was my ninth birthday."

"That's right."

"And you were too chicken to go on with me."

"I was too smart to go on with you. You barfed up the rainbow cotton candy you'd just eaten. It was so gross."

"Rainbow barf!" Cat screamed.

"*Sha*, Catriella. You're giving me a headache," Ms. Wasserman said. "Dinner in two minutes."

"I'll be right there!" Abby called, wishing she could run next door and join them for dinner like she'd done so many times before.

"We'd love to have you, Abigail!" Ms. Wasserman shouted.

"You don't have to yell, Mom. Abby can hear you."

"Okay. I didn't know."

Cat twirled the end of her braid. "Know what you could do that's different for your birthday this year?"

"What?" Abby sat on the floor, leaning against her bed.

"You could talk to that cute boy next door."

"What? I can't." Abby thought of the last time she spoke to him and managed to get out one word before tripping and embarrassing herself. She'd avoided him since.

Cat got closer to the screen. "You can, Abigail Braverman. And you should. It could be like . . . a birthday present to yourself."

Abby thought about it for the thousandth time. She wished she had the courage to talk to him—really talk and have an actual conversation—but she knew she'd somehow mess it up and humiliate herself. "Nope. Nope. And nope times infinity."

"Abby!!!"

"Catriella!"

"Sorry, Mom." Cat whispered, "Our apartment here is

so small, she hears everything. So, what do you think will happen if you talk to him? Your head will explode?"

I'll trip!

"You can do it. And you know what else you could do today?"

Abby rolled her eyes. "What? Run the Boston Marathon? Swim the English Channel? Climb Mount Everest?"

"Nah, those things are child's play compared to this."

"I'm listening."

"When you go to Scoops Ahoy tonight with your moms, you could order a flavor of ice cream besides vanilla. Maybe mint chip. Chocolate marshmallow. Strawberry shortcake. Go wild!"

"Are you bananas? Vanilla's the best flavor. End of story."

"You're hopeless, Abs. You know that, right?"

Abby smiled. She knew.

"Know what else you are?"

"What?"

"Twelve! Woo-hoo!"

"Woo-hoo!" Abby pumped her fist. "Finally caught up to you!"

"You did. Now go have the most amazing day ever."

"Hey, Cat?"

"Yeah?"

"I . . . miss you."

Cat's lower lip quivered. "Yeah, me too."

Ms. Wasserman's eyeball filled the screen again.

Abby pressed herself backward.

"Sorry, Abigail. Catriella needs to hang up now and have dinner."

"Mom!"

"Please give your moms my love, sweetheart. And have a happy birthday."

"I will. Thank—"

The call disconnected.

Ms. Wasserman must have hung up.

The screen went black, but the image of Cat's red-rimmed eyes and quivering lower lip lingered in Abby's mind.

At Scoops Ahoy, after her birthday dinner with her moms, Abby ordered vanilla ice cream, but she also ordered a scoop of mint chip.

"Look at you trying something new," Mama Dee said, pushing her short dark hair behind her right ear and slurping soda from her root beer float. "Attagirl!"

"A whole new you." Mom Rachel nudged Abby's shoulder. "Abby 2.0."

Abby sat taller. Maybe she could be a different kind of person, one who tried new things, felt comfortable in large groups, and made friends easily. Perhaps with Cat gone, Abby could reinvent herself and become new and improved Abby 2.0.

Thinking of the possibilities, Abby put a spoonful of mint chip in her mouth.

The flavor was too strong. The chocolate pieces felt like pebbles on her tongue.

She didn't like it.

0 (1) 0

Back home with the three of them on the couch and a pile of gifts on the living room floor, Mama Dee placed a plastic tiara with fake jewels and the words BIRTHDAY GIRL on top of Abby's head. "There we go."

"It's bedazzled like Miss Lucy's collar," Mom Rachel said. "Now you and Miss Lucy can both be fancy-pants. We didn't bother giving you the tiara while we were out."

"Knew you wouldn't wear it." Mama Dee folded her hands in her lap. "No way would you do that."

Abby wore the tiara only because it was just the three of them and Miss Lucy in the living room, and the moms promised no photos would be taken.

"Speaking of Princess Lucy . . ." Mom Rachel handed Abby a gift. "This one's from her."

Miss Lucy jumped onto the couch and curled up next to Mom Rachel.

"Thanks, Miss Lucy," Abby said. "Wonder if Fudge swam out and got me a birthday present too."

Mom Rachel gave Abby a playful shove.

Abby smiled and opened a package of pencils with dog erasers.

"For school," Mama Dee said.

"Don't remind me."

"But it's seventh grade," Mom Rachel said. "I loved seventh grade."

Abby sighed. "Did you start seventh grade without your best friend?"

"No," Mom Rachel admitted. "I had a bunch of girl-friends back then."

"My point exactly. I only have Cat, and she's not here anymore."

Mama Dee patted Abby's knee. "You'll join some clubs this year, kiddo. You'll make new friends. You've got this, Abigail. Be tough."

I won't do either of those things, Abby thought. *I'm not tough. And I definitely don't have this. But maybe . . . Maybe Abby 2.0 will have this. A new school year. A new me.* The possibility made Abby shiver with excitement.

Mom Rachel thrust a heavy package onto Abby's lap. "This one's from Paul. He got it for you before he left for camp."

Paul never forgot her birthday, even though he was always at camp during it. Abby opened the card first. Inside, it said, *A six-pack for Six-Pack.*

It was a six-pack of root beer.

Mom Rachel shook her head. "That boy's funny even when he's not here."

Abby carried the root beer into the kitchen and made room for it on a shelf in the fridge so it would be cold when she was ready for a treat.

When she got back, Mom Rachel handed Abby a huge package. "This is from us, sweetheart."

Mama Dee leaned back and cracked her neck. "I'm get-ting old."

Mom Rachel poked her. "If you're old, then what am I? I'm four months older than you."

"You're youthful, Rach. And I'm a cranky old woman."

"You're ridiculous," Mom Rachel said. "That's what you are. We're both still young."

"But I'm younger," Abby pointed out. "Sooooo much younger!"

Mama Dee shoved Abby playfully. "Don't rub it in, Miss Smarty-Pants. Open your present so I can see what your mom got you."

Abby smiled and unwrapped the gift. Inside the box were three tops and two pair of jeans, new underwear and socks, and a book—*How to Be Your Best, Boldest Self.*

Abby bit her bottom lip.

"For school," Mom Rachel said.

"Thank you."

"Best year yet." She waved pretend pom-poms at Abby.

"Yup." *Seventh grade without Cat.* "Best year yet."

"Now, that's our girl." Mama Dee gave Abby a tight squeeze.

Abby felt like a fraud inside that squeeze. But she promised herself she'd try.

"Oh, there's one more." Mom Rachel handed Abby another package. "This came for you the other day. We thought we'd save it for your birthday."

When Abby saw that the return address was from Israel, her heart fluttered. "It's from Cat."

Mom Rachel nodded. "That girl wouldn't forget your big day."

"Never," Mama Dee added. "I'll never know how we got

lucky enough to have Miriam and Cat living next door to us. Best neighbors ever."

Mama Dee's words made Abby miss Cat even more, but at least she had a birthday gift from Cat. Abby carefully opened the package and unwrapped the present inside.

It was a beautiful wooden mezuzah with a brightly painted scene of Jerusalem on it. Abby ran her finger over the smooth surface, then peeked at the scroll hidden inside the back under a tiny piece of fabric. "It's perfect."

"It really is," Mom Rachel said. "What a lovely gift."

Abby squeezed the mezuzah, knowing Cat held it in her hands in Israel.

"Do you want to hang it now?" Mom Rachel asked.

"I can grab a hammer and a couple nails from the garage," Mama Dee offered. "I think I have nails the right size to hang it."

Abby knew exactly what she was supposed to do with the mezuzah. Hang it on a doorframe, say the blessing, and live by the tenets written on the tiny scroll inside. If she did those things, the mezuzah would protect her and her family and keep everyone safe and remind them of their commitment to create a Jewish household. Cat had asked Abby why her family never hung a mezuzah on the doorframe of their house, since they celebrated the Jewish holidays. There were five different mezuzahs hanging in Cat's house. Abby never had a good answer for her. They just didn't have one. Now, thanks to Cat, they did. "Um, not right now."

"Okay." Mom Rachel leaned back and kicked off her shoes. "I'm exhausted."

Mama Dee put her hands behind her head. "Me too. Maybe I'm not so old, just pooped."

"That's probably it." Mom Rachel yawned.

Abby hugged her moms, nearly knocking off her BIRTHDAY GIRL tiara. "Thanks for a great day."

"We love you, Abigail Rebecca Braverman," Mama Dee said. "Newly minted twelve-year-old girl of ours."

"With all our hearts." Mom Rachel grabbed Mama Dee's hand. "Aren't we lucky, babe?"

"So lucky. Old. Tired. And incredibly lucky."

Mom Rachel leaned her head on her shoulder. "I could fall asleep right here."

"Me too," Mama Dee murmured.

Abby smiled at her moms, then took her gifts to her room. She tucked the mezuzah into a box under her bed, where she kept important things like the poetry she'd written and the endless afghan she was crocheting. Abby planned to keep Cat's special gift all to herself instead of hanging it up.

She hoped God didn't mind.

Abby went to the kitchen to have one of the root beers from the six-pack Paul got her. It seemed like the perfect way to end her birthday.

Mama Dee was stuffing the last bits of wrapping paper into a bag.

"I'll take it out," Abby volunteered.

"Well, thank you, Abs." Mama Dee handed her the bag. "Trash can's already at the curb. I lugged it out earlier."

Outside, sounds of croaking frogs filled the warm, hazy air. The nearly full moon shone brightly from a cloudless sky.

Abby stuffed the bag into their trash can by the street when she heard a noise from Cat's house. She whirled around, half expecting Cat to come running toward her and tackle her with a hug.

But of course, there was no Cat. No hug.

It was New Boy, wearing a T-shirt, shorts, and basketball sneakers. He was dragging his family's trash can to the curb.

Abby squeezed her hands into fists so tight, her nails bit into her palms. *Oh, please don't let me do anything stupid in front of him.* She remembered Cat telling her she should say hello to him as a birthday present to herself. *Abby 2.0 can do this,* she told herself. *Pretend you're Cat and say something friendly.* Abby planted her feet firmly so she wouldn't trip. "Hey, there!"

The boy looked over.

Abby hunched her shoulders as if she could retract into a human shell.

"Oh, hey." He smiled and waved.

Abby hadn't anticipated him coming over, but he was walking toward her. Now she'd have to talk with him, and she had no idea how she'd manage that without Cat beside her. Every ounce of temporary bravery drained from her body.

The boy stood so close, his cologne made Abby want to sneeze. *Don't sneeze,* she warned herself. *And don't trip.*

Sweat dripped down her sides; she wasn't sure if it was from the heat or from her nervousness.

"So, how old are you?" The boy shifted his weight from one foot to the other.

"Huh?" *What a strange first question*, Abby thought.

The boy pointed to the top of her head.

Abby's hand shot up to discover she was still wearing the silly tiara. She yanked it off, pulling some hair out with it. She resisted the urge to rub her sore scalp and dumped the tiara into the trash can.

"Not a fan of tiaras, huh?"

"Uh, guess not." Abby couldn't believe she'd walked outside wearing that stupid tiara. "I'm twelve. Today. And for the rest of the year. Right?" *Stop talking, Abby! And whatever you do, don't trip again!*

"Well, happy birthday . . ."

Abby waited for him to finish what he was saying but realized he was waiting for her. "Abby," she said. "Abigail. Well, some people call me Abs." *Do not tell him Paul's nickname for you. Whatever you do, don't say that.* "My brother calls me Six-Pack." *Disaster! Abort mission!* Abby wanted to run into the house, dive underneath her turtle-shell afghan from her bubbe, and never resurface, but she knew if she sprinted across the lawn, she'd face-plant in the grass. Again. Abby 2.0 was a terrible idea. Timid turtles weren't meant to be cheery chipmunks. They just weren't.

"Six-Pack? From Abs? That's funny." The boy smiled. It lit up his face. "Should I call you Abby?"

"Uh, okay." *Brilliant. He probably thinks I'm a few IQ points shy of a coconut.*

"I'm Conrad."

Conrad. Conrad and Abby. Abby and Conrad. Heat exploded behind Abby's cheeks. Surely he noticed her face was about to spontaneously combust. *How did Cat manage this talking thing so easily? At school, she always seemed as comfortable talking to the boys as to the girls, even the boys she admitted to having crushes on.*

"You go to Panther Pride Middle?" Conrad pointed down the street, even though the middle school was over a mile away.

Abby nodded.

Conrad tilted back on his heels. "What grade will you be going into?"

"Seventh," Abby croaked past her desert-dry throat. She needed that root beer.

"I'm going into eighth."

He's older.

"Maybe you could show me around when school starts. I know I'm going to get lost. That school's huge."

Abby nodded again. For too long. She felt like a bobble-head doll in the back of a car going over a road with endless speed bumps. Then Abby stopped suddenly because she didn't want Conrad to think she was agreeing that he would get lost, only that she would show him around. And that the school was huge.

Why is socializing so impossible for me?

Conrad leaned a hand on the trash can lid. "Maybe we could walk to school together."

Abby's eyes went as wide as if he'd suggested they get married.

"I mean, if you want to." Conrad's hand slipped off the

trash can lid, and he stumbled. "Um, I . . ."

It made Abby feel better that Conrad stumbled, that she wasn't the only clumsy one. "I'd . . . uh . . ." Abby couldn't get any more words out. It was like the connection between her brain and her mouth broke. It felt like she'd been standing next to Conrad for hours, smelling his intoxicating cologne and being utterly, hopelessly silent. She couldn't endure it another second and ran back into her house as though an alligator were chasing her.

"Um . . . ," he called after her, but Abby didn't turn.

She leaped inside and shut the door behind her. Abby could almost hear Cat calling her a dork and telling her she should have answered Conrad instead of running away.

At least I didn't trip this time. That's an improvement.

Abby peeked out the window next to the door. Conrad was walking back to Cat's house . . . his house. She sank to the floor in the foyer and covered her face with her hands.

"You okay there, cowboy?" Mama Dee asked.

"What?" Abby hadn't realized anyone was sitting there. She stood and brushed off her shorts. "Yeah. I'm fine. Perfect. Why wouldn't I be?"

"Sheesh. All right, then." Mama Dee made a loud noise with her magazine and went back to reading. "You're acting weird, that's all."

Abby flapped her arms like a chicken at her mom. "I'm. Not. Acting. Weird."

"Who said you were?" Mom Rachel asked as she walked into the living room.

"Don't ask," Mama Dee warned her.

Abby threw her hands up in frustration, grabbed a root beer from the fridge, and brought it to her room, where she planned to hide out for the rest of her life.

"I should never have talked to him," Abby told Fudge, who was asleep on his rock. "I'm never going to be able to talk to people easily like Cat does." Abby changed into pajamas, got into bed, and pulled her afghan all the way up to her chin. "I should stop trying. I keep embarrassing myself."

She replayed her interactions with Conrad over in her mind on an endless loop. Abby thought of the things she could have said, like *I'd love to walk to school together.* Then she remembered the dumb barely-words she'd actually said. And the times she was quiet as a stone when she should have talked.

Fudge was still on his rock. She was able to see him clearly in the full moon's light streaming into her room through the partially open blinds.

"Turtles are supposed to be quiet," she whispered to Fudge. "It's when turtles try to be playful otters or barking seals that trouble starts. Why can't the rest of the world appreciate turtles for exactly who they are?"

Abby kissed her fingertips and touched Fudge's warm shell. "Good night. I appreciate you for exactly who you are."

She was sure Fudge opened his mouth and smiled.

Friday the 13th—Unlucky, Lucky, and Unlucky

About a week and a half later, on the day Paul was coming home from camp, Abby had the Monopoly board set up with his favorite snacks nearby—Doritos and Twizzlers. She made limeade spritzers garnished with mint leaves from Mom's kitchen garden box. Abby decided not to go with Mom Rachel to pick up Paul from camp so she'd have time to get everything ready for his homecoming.

When the car pulled into the driveway, Abby flung open the door and kept Miss Lucy back with her foot. *Paul is home. Everything will be better.*

Mom Rachel got out of the car first, went to the trunk, and hauled Paul's huge duffel bag to the door.

"Where's Paul?"

Mom Rachel turned back to the car. "He's . . ." She rushed over, knocked on the car window, and opened the door. "He fell asleep," she called. "I guess being a counselor-in-training wore him out."

Abby bit her bottom lip as she watched her brother drag himself from the car, shoulders slumped. Paul usually bounded home from camp, excited to talk about all the things he did, even if he was worn out.

"Hey, Six-Pack," Paul said with the energy of a soggy cornflake.

"What's wrong?" Abby asked.

Mom Rachel hoisted the duffel bag and brushed past her. "He's just tired, Abigail."

Abby looked at Paul for confirmation.

He nodded and walked in.

She followed them inside, sure that when Paul saw the Monopoly game and his favorite snacks on the table, he'd perk up.

Miss Lucy jumped all over Paul's legs and yipped and whined like she hadn't seen him in a thousand years.

He bent to pet her, then glanced at the game. "Oh, that's sweet, Abs. Maybe later. Okay?"

"But, Paul . . ." They were supposed to play Monopoly all afternoon. It was Friday; school started on Monday. Abby knew Paul would be too busy to play games with her once school started. Plus, he's the one who asked her to have it set up when he got home.

Paul was already halfway to his room.

"I didn't play your banjo," she said softly.

The only response she heard was the sound of her brother's bedroom door closing.

0 0 0

While her mom puttered around the kitchen, Abby grabbed the house key from the hook and slipped outside, quiet as a turtle.

Humidity engulfed her as she walked to the neighborhood park, which had a red-clay walking trail, a small pond, a basketball court, picnic tables, and a playground.

Abby sat on an uncomfortable metal bench facing the pond, where she and Cat used to look for alligators and talk about important things, like where they wanted to volunteer when they were old enough (an animal shelter for Cat and the public library for Abby) and who was crush-worthy in their classes (nearly every boy for Cat and nearly no one for Abby). The last conversation they'd had on that bench was when Cat told Abby she and her mom were moving to Israel. Abby wondered if the bench was cursed.

"Hey there, Six-Pack!"

Abby turned, expecting to see Paul back to himself and ready to play Monopoly with her.

It took a second for Abby's brain to process that it wasn't Paul walking toward the bench. It was Conrad, wearing black shorts and a red T-shirt with a basketball tucked under his arm. He was grinning, until he wasn't. "Um, sorry. I meant Abby. Abigail?"

Abby stared at him, wide-eyed.

"Abs? Help me out here."

Abby's internal furnace blasted heat into her cheeks. She wondered if she'd ever get better at this socializing thing, if Abby 2.0 would suddenly kick in one day and this would get easier. "Any name is fine." *I don't want him calling me Six-Pack. That would be endlessly embarrassing.* "I mean, Abby is good. Yeah, Abby. Well, whatever you want." *Shut up already!* "But Abby is nice."

"Abby *is* nice."

The internal furnace inside Abby's face ratcheted up approximately ten million degrees. If she stayed next to Conrad like this, she'd turn into a pile of smoldering ash.

Conrad held out the basketball. "Want to play?"

She pointed to herself.

"Yeah. You ever play?"

Abby channeled her inner Cat. Confident Cat. Abby had played basketball once in PE class and jammed her finger so badly, it hurt for a week, but Conrad didn't need to know that. "Yup."

"Cool. There's never anyone out here to shoot hoops with."

Abby followed Conrad to the court. She felt absolutely confident . . . that she'd humiliate herself.

After one game of HORSE, during which Abby quickly received the letters *H-O-R-S-E*, despite Conrad obviously missing a bunch of shots on purpose, it was clear Abby had not improved since that one game in PE class. At least she didn't injure herself this time.

Conrad ran a hand through his sweaty brown hair. "Um, maybe we should do something else."

"I stink at basketball."

"You're okay."

"No, I'm terrible."

Conrad kicked at the ground. "Yeah, you're really bad. When you missed that one shot, I thought the ball would go over the fence and into the pond."

"Yeah, and it would probably bonk an alligator on the head."

Conrad smiled. "Or knock an osprey out of the sky."

Abby squinted up. "Or bump into a satellite."

They were walking toward the playground. "Or bounce around on the moon."

"No gravity. Those would be some big bounces," Abby said.

Conrad laughed, and Abby realized she was making conversation. She made him laugh. Maybe this Abby 2.0 thing might work out after all.

"Want to swing?" Conrad asked. "There aren't any little kids around."

Abby hadn't swung in years. She and Cat used to have competitions to see who could swing higher. Cat always won. "Okay."

"Let's see who can get higher," Conrad said, pumping his legs and leaning back hard.

Abby pumped her legs too, until she was nearly as high as he was, but she didn't like the feeling of her stomach dropping each time she went up, so she allowed herself to slow. "How's the view from up there?" she called, hoping to be funny.

The sound of Conrad's laugh made Abby feel like she'd scored a metaphorical basket.

Conrad flew off the swing, windmilling his arms until he landed in a crouch on the wood chips.

Abby slowed, then stopped herself with her feet and climbed off.

When they walked home together, Conrad invited her over to his house for something to drink.

To Cat's house.

Abby knew she should ask her moms first, but she also didn't want to seem like a baby. "Is your mom home?" she asked, knowing her moms wouldn't want her visiting Conrad without an adult there.

Conrad checked his phone. "She should be home from work soon."

What would Cat do?

"If you don't . . ." Conrad started to say.

"Sure."

Conrad's face brightened. "Oh, okay. Cool."

He opened the red door of the avocado-green house and tossed his basketball onto the floor.

The first thing Abby noticed was that the mezuzah was gone from the doorframe. There were two tiny holes where the nails had been. Cat's mom must have taken down the mezuzah before they moved. She must have removed all the mezuzahs from their house before they left.

It was strange for Abby to be in the house without Cat and her mom there. The furniture was the same, but there was a sports blanket thrown over the side of the couch. There were a couple pairs of sneakers and flip-flops in the foyer, which Ms. Wasserman never would have allowed. She liked things neat. The house even smelled different, like some stinky pine-scented air freshener instead of Ms. Wasserman's cooking.

"I'm going to throw on a clean T-shirt," Conrad said. "Kitchen's back there."

Abby knew where the kitchen was. She sat at the table in a swivel chair and looked for things that were different. It reminded her of the puzzles in *Highlights for Children* where you had to figure out what was wrong with the picture, like a skunk sitting on a dinner plate or a sneaker on a bookshelf. In the kitchen, there was a dish towel hanging on the stove that read, DINNER IS READY WHEN THE SMOKE ALARM GOES OFF; there was a bright orange blender on the counter that didn't belong to Ms. Wasserman; and there were chili pepper lights strung around the kitchen—fun, but definitely not Cat's mom's taste. Abby felt like she'd entered an alternate universe in which Cat's house wasn't quite her house.

"Do you drink tea?"

Conrad had startled Abby.

"My uncle taught me that when you're really hot, you should drink something warm. It makes your body cool off. He's a chef and works in hot kitchens, so he knows."

Abby nodded. She wanted to tell Conrad her moms worked in kitchens too—that they used to work in a fancy restaurant in the city together—but she kept quiet and took it all in.

Conrad filled a teapot with water. "Peppermint tea okay?"

Who was this boy?

"Sounds good." Abby assumed Conrad would use a tea bag, not fresh mint leaves, like Mom Rachel used when she brewed mint tea.

Conrad did use tea bags to make two mugs of tea that he brought to the table along with a plate of mint Milano cookies. "It's a theme snack," Conrad said. "Mint."

Abby blinked at him, wondering if this was what it was like to date a boy. The boys at school seemed so rough and gruff, always shoving one another and laughing too loud, but Conrad was thoughtful and sensitive. Would he act differently at school, or was this how he was all the time? Abby couldn't wait to tell Cat about him. Maybe she'd even write a poem about Conrad when she got home. About the way his soft brown hair fell over one eye. About the way his warm voice sent vibrations down her spine. About his gentleness.

Conrad sat in the swivel chair beside Abby and took a cookie. "So, do you walk to school, or does someone drive you?"

"I walk. It's only about a mile." Abby nibbled the edge of her cookie to make sure she liked it. The vanilla cookie part was good, but the chocolate-mint filling was too tingly on her tongue. She swallowed it anyway and left the rest of the cookie on a napkin.

"Do you want to walk together on Monday?"

Abby coughed.

"You okay?"

She felt her face redden but managed to nod.

The front door opened, and Abby stiffened.

"Hey, Ma!" Conrad called. "I'm in here with Abby from next door."

A woman wearing black slacks and a white button-down shirt walked in. Her blond hair was up in a ponytail. There were dark circles under her eyes. "Hi there, Abby." She stuck out her hand. "I'm Ms. Miller, Conrad's mom."

Abby grabbed the woman's slender hand and shook, like Mama Dee taught her. Strong grip. Firm shake. Make eye contact. The eye contact part was hard for Abby, but she did it anyway.

"I think I saw you with your mom and brother the other day. I'm sorry I haven't stopped by to say hello. Been pulling extra shifts at the diner, but I look forward to meeting your mom and dad." Then she turned to Conrad. "We need to get you some school clothes, bud. School starts in three days." She grabbed a cookie. "Mmm. My favorite."

"Moms," Abby blurted.

Ms. Miller turned back to Abby. "Huh?"

"We're a two-mom family."

"Oh, then I'm looking forward to meeting your moms."

Abby felt her shoulders relax.

At the door, when Abby was leaving, Conrad asked, "Want me to call a Lyft to take you home?"

Abby burst out laughing. *He's funny, like Paul.*

"It'll be a challenge," Abby said. "But I think I can make it across the lawn to my house."

"Let me give you my number in case you run into trouble."

Abby's whole body shivered. *He wants to give me his number! Wait till I tell Cat!*

Conrad put his number into Abby's phone. "Call me, then I'll have yours."

She did.

Conrad leaned against the wall. "See you for school Monday."

He looked so relaxed and comfortable. All the connections in Abby's brain were misfiring. "Monday. School," she managed.

Conrad laughed. "You okay?"

"Mm-hmm." Abby held her phone for a few extra seconds before putting it into her pocket.

When Abby opened the door to her house, Mom Rachel was on the couch reading a cookbook. She lowered it. "Where'd you go? I finished making the fettuccine, and you weren't here."

"Oh, I ended up going to the park and then over to Conrad's house." Abby said it like it was no big deal, but her heart knew it was a very big deal. It was her first time going over to a boy's house . . . and getting his number . . . and they would be walking to school together Monday.

Mom Rachel arched her eyebrows. "Over to Conrad's house?"

"Mm-hmm."

"It would've been nice if you'd told me." Mom Rachel

closed the cookbook and laid it aside. "As in, Abigail Braverman, it would have been nice if you'd *asked* if you could go over there. I didn't know where you were. It's not safe to go over to some boy's house. We don't know him."

It was Cat's house, Abby wanted to say. "Mom, he served me mint tea and cookies. I don't think there was anything to worry about. And it was only a few minutes before his mom was there."

"You went over to his house when his mom wasn't there? Abigail!"

"What did you think would happen?" Abby plopped onto the edge of the couch, far away from the stare her mom leveled at her. "Sorry. I'll tell you next time."

"You'll . . ."

"Ask."

"Better."

Mama Dee came into the living room, drying her hair with a towel. "I had rainbow sprinkles in my hair today, icing in my left eyebrow, and chocolate smears on both elbows. It was like a rainbow unicorn cupcake exploded all over me."

Mom Rachel laughed.

Mama Dee sat close to Mom Rachel and put the towel on her lap. "Now that our girl is home, can we please eat that delicious-looking dinner you made? I'm starving. Woman can't live on unicorn cupcakes alone, you know."

Mom Rachel leaned over and kissed Mama Dee on the cheek. "It's all ready."

When a door opened, everyone looked up.

Paul walked into the living room. His hair was flat and greasy. His clothes looked like they'd been stuffed into the bottom of a hamper for a week, and he smelled like a mixture of campfire and body odor. "Moms?"

"Yes?" Mom Rachel and Mama Dee said at the same time.

Paul squeezed his hands into fists. "I need to tell you something."

The Beginning of Everything

O n Monday, Abby woke way before her alarm.

Her first thoughts were of Paul. He didn't let Abby stay and listen when he talked to the moms on Friday. And even though she left the door to her bedroom open and strained to hear, they spoke in such hushed tones, she couldn't decipher any of their conversation, only the worried sounds of their voices.

Abby had asked her moms what he'd said, but they'd told her it was private for right now. So Abby spent the weekend with her imagination going wild with possibilities. Did Paul catch an incurable disease at camp? Had he witnessed a crime? Was he planning to move to another state to finish high school at some fancy private school, far away from them?

Whatever it was, the moms had been on edge all weekend. And Paul had spent a lot of time in his room with the door closed. Abby didn't hear him playing his banjo even once. This, she knew, was not a good sign.

Abby's stomach squeezed with thoughts of Conrad, too.

He would be coming over to her house soon, and they would be walking to school together. There were so many things that could go wrong.

Abby pictured Conrad, his brown hair falling over one eye and the relaxed way he looked at her. Her heart thumped.

She grabbed her journal and poured her nervous energy into a poem.

C-O-N-R-A-D

Cute. Cuter. Cutest.
Offers *mint tea and a quiet smile.*
Nerd?
R *adiates . . . gentleness and kindness.*
An eighth grader *who . . .*
Deserves *further study!*

Writing the poem took Abby's mind off worrying, but once she put her journal away, the nervousness came back with a vengeance. She couldn't eat breakfast. All Abby could do as she waited for Conrad to arrive was chew her fingernails and work on crocheting her endless afghan, which spilled over her lap and the edge of the bed and onto the floor. Soon it would be expanding right out the door! Abby might feel better if she at least knew what was going on with her brother, why everyone was so anxious.

When there was a knock at the door, Abby gasped, ran to the door, took a deep breath, and opened it.

Conrad tugged on his button-down short-sleeved shirt, as though he'd be more comfortable wearing a T-shirt. "Hi."

Abby gave a little wave and noticed one of her nail beds was bleeding. She put that hand behind her back. "Hey."

Conrad pushed his hair out of his eye, but it flopped back down. "You ready?"

Abby nodded, even though that felt like a lie. She knew she'd never be ready for this. She smoothed down her new purple T-shirt with blue trim around the sleeves and neckline. First days of school had so many unexpected things to navigate, so many challenging variables to figure out. Anything could go wrong at any moment. And she didn't have Cat to be a buffer, a bridge.

"Mom, we're leaving!" Abby called, expecting Mom Rachel to rush out from the kitchen to take photos, hand her a lunch packed with treats she and Mama Dee made the night before, and give her last-minute advice about being open to new experiences so she could make friends, blah, blah, blah.

But Mom Rachel didn't come rushing out from the kitchen. She didn't take photos. She didn't give her lunch or advice.

Abby heard her mom on the phone making a doctor's appointment for Paul, which caused Abby's stomach to squeeze into a knot of worry. So the something wrong with Paul was medical. Maybe he did catch some scary disease at camp. Would she catch it too?

"Ready?" Conrad asked again.

She shook her head to pull herself out of her own worrisome thoughts. "Yup."

As they walked down the street, Abby took a moment to realize that even though she wasn't walking to school with her best friend, she wasn't alone, like she'd expected to be. She was walking beside Conrad Miller, and that felt like something surprising and good.

Her Bubbe Marcia—Mom Rachel's mother—sometimes said, *When a door closes, a window opens. So don't look so long at the closed door that you miss the open window.* Abby never really understood what that meant, but Cat moving away this summer felt like a door slamming shut, and Conrad moving in was like a window opening . . . and a peppermint-scented breeze wafting through.

Abby pulled her shoulders back and held her head high. This moment felt kind of amazing, but it would have been even better if it weren't mixed with anxiety about the first day of school and worry for what was going on with Paul. She was determined to figure out the medical mystery, but first she had to get through the school day. And she wasn't sure if she'd manage to get through it as Abby 2.0 or plain old Abby.

She'd forgotten how loud the courtyard full of kids was before school. She could hear it all the way across the street, where they were waiting for the crossing guard to give them the signal to go. The shrieking and yelling felt like a metal grater rubbing against Abby's brain—the exact opposite of the feeling she got when she explored the trails at Winding

River Park, her favorite place in all of Port Paradise. Abby was pretty sure she'd get through this day as plain old Abby, who wished she were back home in her quiet room with Fudge, her journal, and her endless afghan to work on.

When she and Conrad entered the noisy, crowded courtyard, they staked out a spot off to the side, near the fence, as far away from everyone as they could get.

Conrad put his hands over his ears. "This place is way bigger than my other school."

Abby nodded, hoping he'd take his hands away from his ears because someone would make fun of him if he didn't.

Conrad jammed his hands into his pockets and hunched forward.

Abby scanned the crowd.

Girls were hugging one another and asking about one another's summer. No one hugged Abby. No one asked about her summer.

Abby crossed her arms tightly over her chest, even though Mom Rachel once told her it made her look unapproachable and unfriendly. It was all the protective shell she had today, and she was using it.

She moved closer to Conrad because he was quiet and his face looked pale. "It'll be okay," she said softly, realizing she was talking to herself as much as to him, and her words were more hope than fact.

He nodded but looked like he didn't quite believe her.

A loud buzz cut through the chatter, and everyone funneled into the cafeteria through double doors. There, students sat on the benches of long rectangular tables while the principal gave a talk that involved words like "pride" and "respect" and "responsibility."

Then students lined up to get their class schedules and go to their first-period classes. Today classes were shortened and it was an early release, so students would have an opportunity to meet their teachers, learn some of the expectations, and not do much else.

Tomorrow would be the first full day of classes.

After Abby got her schedule, she found Conrad in the crush of kids and helped him navigate the crowded halls to get to his first class.

At the doorway of the classroom, Conrad turned and looked at Abby. His Adam's apple moved up and down as he swallowed. "I'll wait for you after school by the fence." Then he slipped inside the classroom.

As Abby moved among a whole ocean of jostling, chattering kids, she lamented that not a single one of them was Catriella Robyn Wasserman.

In her first period class, Abby sat in the back row and turned to the second page in her spiral notebook. She thought she might write another poem but ended up making a list instead, which was kind of like a poem.

First Day of School:
1. 7th grade without Cat
2. Cat was the social glue that connected me to other people.

3. She was the binding agent, like we learned about in science class last year.
4. No binding agent, no connection
5. Something is wrong with Paul.
6. This stinks.

When Miranda Gross, a girl who was in all Abby's classes last year, sat next to her, Abby slammed her spiral notebook closed. No one needed to read her list, especially Miranda.

Miranda nodded in her direction, and Abby felt a flicker of hope. Maybe Miranda grew nicer over the summer. Perhaps they might become friends this year. Abby could use a friend. Cat used to talk to Miranda about nail polish colors, hairstyles, and clothes. Sometimes Abby joined their conversations, but she found those subjects boring; plus, she hated when Miranda made fun of other kids for how they dressed or acted. Abby thought Miranda might be making fun of her behind her back too.

"I heard Cat moved to Israel," Miranda said. "You must miss her. You two were, like, always together."

Abby hadn't expected anyone to talk to her about Cat. Honestly, she hadn't expected anyone to talk to her at all. She didn't know how to respond, or even if she should. If she talked about Cat right now, she might cry, and that absolutely could not happen on the first day of school. Or any day of school. Tears in middle school were like blood in water filled with sharks.

"Okay then." Miranda turned the other way and started

a conversation with Laura Fournier, another girl who was in all of Abby's classes last year.

Laura and Miranda suddenly laughed.

Abby was pretty sure they were laughing at her.

She turned forward, realizing she probably wasn't going to make any new friends this year.

At the end of the school day, Abby burst through the exit doors into the warm, steamy air and bright sunshine. She found Conrad leaning against the fence where they stood before school started.

She almost walked past him, thinking he couldn't really be waiting there for her—the girl who sat by herself in the cafeteria, at the end of a table near a smelly trash can. The girl who tripped in the hallway on the way to French class. *Très klutzy!* The girl who spoke to no one other than responding to each of her teachers with a quiet "here" when they took roll.

"Hey!" Conrad smiled and waved.

Every molecule inside Abby jumped for joy. He did wait for her. "Hi!"

As they walked toward home together, the protective shell Abby had cast in ice around her heart melted away.

"Everything go okay today?" Conrad asked.

Abby nodded, even though it wasn't true. "How was your first day of eighth grade?"

"I only got lost three times."

He said it in such a sweet, hopeful way that Abby couldn't help but laugh. "Only three?"

"Mm-hmm. Would have been four, but you helped me find my first class."

Abby loved how their steps matched each other's almost the whole way home, and she imagined their heartbeats were in perfect rhythm too.

Abby hoped Conrad would invite her in again for mint tea, but he said, "See you tomorrow," when they got to their houses. "I'll come to your house again in the morning."

Abby nodded.

Inside, she went straight to the kitchen, dropped her notebook and pen on the counter, and sat on a stool facing her mom.

Mom Rachel was chopping sweet potatoes with a small cleaver. Her wild black hair was up in a ponytail. She wore light blue overalls and a purple T-shirt with a unicorn on the front. Abby liked that she and her mom were both wearing purple T-shirts.

"Hey, Abs." Mom Rachel put the cleaver down. "So?"

Abby realized her throat was desert-dry. "Can I have a seltzer?"

Mom Rachel grabbed the bottle of homemade raspberry seltzer and poured Abby a glass. She plucked a couple mint leaves off a plant on the counter to throw on top. "How was your first day . . . without Cat?"

Abby took a sip of fizzy seltzer, glad her mom recognized that it would be hard for her today. "It was okay, I guess. I liked walking with Conrad, but I'm worried about Paul. I don't like being left out of things."

"Oh, sweetie. I know. He's got a doctor's appointment in two days. I'm sure we'll learn more then. Until that time, let's try not to worry."

Mom Rachel went back to whacking sweet potatoes into small cubes. She was usually very calm when working in the kitchen, but she chopped those potatoes ferociously, like she was hacking at something else.

"You seem worried," Abby said.

Her mom looked up. "To be honest, I'm a little worried, but I'm hoping it's nothing and he'll be fine." She looked at Paul's closed bedroom door. "He's in his room now, resting. School must have worn him out."

Or maybe it was something more than school that wore him out. Abby wished she knew what that was, what her mom wasn't telling her. She had a nagging feeling she should have put that mezuzah up the moment she got it.

Abby knocked on Paul's bedroom door.

"Enter!"

Her brother was in bed, his back against the wall as he quietly plucked his banjo.

This made Abby's heart happy.

"Listen to this, Abs."

She sat on his desk chair and scooped Miss Lucy onto her lap, since she'd followed her into his room.

Paul played a fun riff. "Just came up with that. What'd you think?"

Abby made Miss Lucy's front paws clap.

Moving his banjo out of the way, Paul bowed his head, took off his three steel finger picks, and dropped them onto the corner of his desk. "How was your first day, Six-Pack?"

Abby petted Miss Lucy's long, silky ears. "No one really talked to me."

Paul sat forward. "Did *you* talk to anyone?"

"No."

"Six-Pack?"

"Yeah?"

"You've got to give a little."

"It's hard."

"I know."

But Abby doubted Paul understood. He was an extrovert. Being social was easy for Paul, and he already had two best friends, Jake and Ethan, to do everything with. Paul was not a turtle. He was an otter. Otters were fun and outgoing. Everyone loved otters.

"How was your day?" Abby asked, hoping he'd tell her about more than school.

"Hard."

"The first day?"

"Yeah, I've got chem, pre-calc, advanced history. Crazy difficult stuff. Plus I have to start looking at colleges. And preparing for the SATs. And . . ." He scratched his elbow, but didn't say anything else.

"Paul?"

"Yeah?"

Abby put Miss Lucy back on the floor because her nails

were digging into Abby's legs. "What's going on . . . with you?"

"It's probably nothing, Six-Pack."

Abby stared at him.

"I have to go to a doctor to check something out. I'll tell you if it's anything to worry about."

"You sound like Mom." Abby chewed on a thumbnail. "Are you worried?"

"Of course I'm worried. I'm Jewish and neurotic."

Abby burst out laughing. Her brother could always make her laugh. "Paul?"

"What's up?"

"Love you."

"Aw man." Paul got up, spun his sister on the chair, then gave her an awkward hug, his bony body pressing into hers. "Love you too, weirdo."

Happy New Year, My Foot!

Three weeks later, the first day of Rosh Hashanah, the Jewish New Year, was Monday, the same day as Paul's appointment with the urologist.

"Tell me again what this doctor does," Abby said to Mom Rachel in the kitchen early that morning. The whole house smelled of dill, onion, and garlic from the big pot of soup bubbling on the stove.

Mom Rachel rushed around the kitchen, putting dishes into the fridge and taking others out.

"Abby, I already told you. Paul's regular doctor said he had to go to a specialist called a urologist."

"What will the urologist do?"

Mom Rachel put a large ceramic bowl in front of Abby along with a plate. "Here, at least help while we talk."

Forming matzo balls for the soup was Abby's favorite holiday job. She washed her hands, then pressed the mixture of matzo meal, water, oil, and eggs into meatball-size spheres by rolling them between her palms.

Her mom, meanwhile, chopped carrots for the tzimmes, a stew made with root vegetables and sweet dried fruit. "Paul's doctor sent him to get a blood test and something called an ultrasound."

Abby nodded while she kept rolling the mixture into matzo balls.

Mom Rachel blew a few stray strands of hair that had come loose from her ponytail out of her eye. "We did all that already, then later today we'll go to the urologist, and he'll tell us the test results."

Abby looked at her mom. "You seem nervous."

"I'm—ouch!" Mom Rachel stuck her knuckle into her mouth. "See what you made me do?"

Abby leaned back. "What *I* made you do?"

"Sorry, sweetheart. I'm a little stressed with the big dinner and . . . everything. Let me go put a Band-Aid on this thing." She went into her bedroom and closed the door.

Abby kept shaping matzo balls, but she knew her mom wasn't telling the truth. Cooking never made Mom Rachel stressed. It relaxed her. The kitchen was her mom's Zen zone. She was obviously nervous about going to this new doctor with Paul, which made Abby's stomach tighten with worry too.

Paul seemed fine. What could be wrong with him?

After Abby shaped all the matzo balls for the soup and helped her mom finish the carrot tzimmes, she went to her room and spent time with Fudge. She hadn't been paying much attention to him lately.

"Hey, little buddy." Abby put her face close to the tank and watched the water distort Fudge's world. "Happy New Year."

Fudge seemed unimpressed about the holiday.

Abby checked her phone, hoping there would be something exciting, like a text from Conrad.

There wasn't.

But there was one from Cat.

Shanah Tovah to you and your family.

Abby replied.

> **Happy New Year. Hope you have a**
> **nice celebration there with your mom.**

Cat responded right away.

We're celebrating with people from my mom's work ...
like, right now. I should NOT be on the phone. Hahaha.
Love you, Abs.

Abby held the phone to her heart.

> **Love you too, Cat.**

"All is well," Abby told Fudge. "Cat is still my best friend. Zeyde Jordan and Bubbe Marcia will be here later today, and I can finally show Bubbe how big my endless afghan has grown since she last saw it."

Fudge came close to the glass of the tank and looked at Abby.

"And I have a feeling Paul will get good news from this special doctor today so Mom Rachel can stop worrying, and everything can go back to normal."

Fudge swam away from Abby as though he didn't believe a word she said.

Later, in the kitchen, Mama Dee tucked her white button-down shirt into black slacks and slipped an apron over her head. "Abby, you'd better leave room for dessert tonight. I'm making an apple cake."

Mom Rachel bumped into Mama Dee's hip. "She's adding the fancy Penzeys Ceylon Cinnamon. Yum!"

Abby loved watching the two of them in the kitchen together. They seemed so happy. Mom Rachel's groovy vibe loosened up Mama Dee's more serious self.

"That's not all." Mama Dee held up a finger. "There will also be ruglock."

"That's not how you say it." Mom Rachel shook her head. "It's rugelach."

"That's what I said—ruglock." Mama Dee winked at Abby. "Don't worry. It'll taste good. That's all that matters."

Mom Rachel put a soup ladle in front of Mama Dee's mouth, as though it were a microphone. "And now, for the best dessert of all." Mama Dee nodded toward Abby. "Drumroll, please, Abs."

Abby was glad Mom Rachel seemed so much more relaxed than earlier. Abby used her fingers as drumsticks on the counter to create a drumroll for Mama Dee's big announcement.

"Challah bread pudding." Mama Dee made an exaggerated bow. "My Rosh Hashanah dessert game is on point this year. Not bad for a shiksa, eh?"

"Dee!" Mom Rachel whapped her with a kitchen towel. "You'd better get busy, or we'll be eating plain bread for dessert." Mom Rachel paused, then looked panicked. "Oh no."

"What's wrong?" Abby feared her mom just remembered some awful thing that had to do with her brother.

"We almost forgot the tashlik ceremony."

"Oh." Abby let out a relieved breath and scrambled off the stool. "I'll get Paul."

"I'll grab the bread for the ceremony," Mama Dee said.

Abby knocked on Paul's bedroom door, but he didn't answer, so she whispered, "Paul?"

Mom Rachel put a hand on Abby's shoulder. "Why don't we let him be?"

Abby whirled to face her mom. "Paul always goes with us."

"I know, but . . ."

Mom Rachel guided Abby away from Paul's room, and they met Mama Dee, who was waiting at the front door with a small bag of bread.

Abby looked back toward Paul's room, then the three of them walked to the pond at the park.

"It doesn't feel right without Paul here," Abby said quietly.

Both her moms put an arm around her shoulders.

Each of them took a few pieces of bread from the bag Mama Dee held. The bread was supposed to represent their sins from the past year.

"This is one of my favorite traditions," Mama Dee whispered in a solemn tone.

Mom Rachel said the prayer, and they cast their sins—the bread—into the water.

Then they walked home, all holding sweaty hands with one another.

Abby felt lighter, but Paul's absence from the tashlik ceremony increased her worry about what might be going on with him. If she weren't holding her moms' hands, she would have crossed her fingers, hoping the specialist Paul was going to see later today would tell them everything's okay—and that they will have a sweet new year.

A couple hours later, Mom Rachel gave Mama Dee instructions on when to warm up each of the dishes she'd made. "I hope we're back before Mom and Dad come, but you know how these specialists can keep you waiting forever."

Mama Dee, both taller and wider than Mom Rachel, enveloped her in a hug that looked like she'd swallowed her up. "You take care of our boy. Abby and I will take care of everything here."

Mom Rachel nodded.

Miss Lucy barked.

"You, too, Miss Lucy." Mama Dee bent and gave her a scratch behind the ears.

Mom Rachel looked over at Paul. "Ready for this, bud?"

Paul, long and lanky, stood taller than both of his moms. "Nah. Definitely not ready for this." He faced Abby. "Leave some matzo balls for me, Six-Pack."

"I'll try," Abby said. "You know I love me some matzo balls."

"I do." Paul winked at Abby before they left.

As soon as the front door closed, Mama Dee turned to Abby, cracked her knuckles, and then went into full panic mode. "Okay, Abs. I'll need your help."

Miss Lucy looked out the window beside the door and whined.

"Don't need your help, Miss Lucy." Then in a deep voice, she said, "Go to your bed."

Miss Lucy trotted over to her bed in the great room and plopped down with a huff.

Abby knew Miss Lucy would have never listened to her if she had told her to go to her bed. Mama Dee had a voice you paid attention to.

"Your grandparents will be here before we know it. Set up the table with the extra leaf in the middle. Pull out the good plates from the cabinet. And get a salad ready with the things your mom left in the vegetable bin in the fridge."

Abby nodded. "Got it."

"Good. I'm going to get some pots going on the stove,

put a couple things in the oven, and finish up my desserts. Go, team!" Mama Dee extended her fist.

They fist-bumped and got to work.

There was no time to worry about what might happen with Paul at the specialist's office.

"Abigail, get the door!" Mama Dee yelled from her bedroom. "I'm almost finished getting ready."

Abby skidded to the foyer and yanked open the door.

"*Bubbelah*!" Bubbe Marcia squeezed Abby's cheeks between her warm palms. "Look at this *shayna punim*!"

Abby allowed her grandmother's loving words to fill her up. She hugged her petite, gray-haired bubbe until Zeyde Jordan gently moved Bubbe Marcia aside. "You're blocking the way. Let me get to the world's best granddaughter." He hugged Abby and rocked her back and forth, then dug into his pocket and handed Abby a twenty-dollar bill. "There's one for your brother, too. Where's my Paulie?"

"Marcia! Jordan!" Mama Dee came out to the living room wearing navy slacks with a plaid, short-sleeved button-down shirt she was tucking into the waistband, and the hug-fest started over. "Please sit," Mama Dee said. "Can I get you some water? Seltzer?"

When Mama Dee went into the kitchen to get drinks, Abby dashed in and whispered, "Do they know what's going on with Paul?"

Mama Dee nodded. "Here. Bring these out and entertain them. I have to finish getting things ready. Was hoping your mom and Paul would be back by now. Guess they got stuck waiting for that specialist."

Bubbe Marcia reached into a bag and pulled out her crochet project—a scarf she was going to send to her friend Adele, who lived in New Jersey. "I hope I get this done and sent before the weather gets cold up there. How's your endless afghan coming along, Abigail?"

"I can't wait to show you!" Abby ran to her bedroom, dove under her bed, and grabbed the huge afghan. Back in the living room, she held it up so her bubbe could see how much it had grown.

"Oh my word, Abigail. You've been busy. And look at all those colors!"

Abby beamed. "We can crochet together now."

Bubbe patted the seat beside her on the couch. "Sounds perfect, *bubbelah*."

"And I'll twiddle my thumbs over here," Zeyde complained.

Bubbe Marcia playfully slapped Zeyde's knee. "Jordan, behave yourself. We don't have to entertain you."

"Pfft. Entertain, shmentertain. I'm hungry, Marcia." He hollered into the kitchen, "When are we going to eat, Dee? I skipped lunch so I'd have a big appetite for dinner."

Bubbe Marcia patted his belly. "You can afford to skip lunch."

He turned away from her. "Who asked you?"

Bubbe Marcia grinned and went back to crocheting.

"I can bring you a snack, Jordan," Mama Dee called. "While we wait for Rach and Paul."

Bubbe Marcia piped up. "He doesn't need a snack. It will ruin his appetite for dinner."

"It's a big dinner!" Mama Dee yelled. "Lots of courses. Including desserts!"

Zeyde Jordan loosened his belt.

"What're you doing?" Bubbe Marcia asked.

"I'm preparing for the big meal. And desserts."

"You're *meshuga*, you know that? And you drive me *meshuga* too!"

Zeyde Jordan leaned back and folded his hands across his stomach. "I do know that."

Bubbe Marcia shook her head, but her fingers kept moving along the rows of the scarf she was creating.

Abby smiled at her grandparents' banter. They'd been married fifty years, and Abby wanted to be like them if she got married—always able to poke fun at each other and laugh about things.

"So, Abigail, who are you making your endless afghan for?" Bubbe Marcia asked. "Your friend who moved to Israel?"

Abby hadn't thought of sending it to Cat. She hadn't thought about finishing it at all. She just planned to keep working on it. "I don't know yet who it'll be for."

"She's making it for a giant, that's who," Zeyde said.

Bubbe Marcia poked him in the side. "Nobody asked you."

Mama Dee made a lot of noise in the kitchen—the fridge door kept opening and closing, plates were being put on the counter, and the water was running in the sink.

Bubbe Marcia called, "Can I help, Dee?"

"All good in here," Mama Dee responded. "Miss Lucy is my faithful, if not slightly annoying, assistant. You all relax out there."

Bubbe kept crocheting, her chin bobbing slightly with each new stitch.

"Did you hear the one about the pencil?" Zeyde asked.

Abby shook her head. Her fingers moved fast and furious with the crochet hook, but not nearly as fast as Bubbe's fingers with their swollen knuckles.

"Never mind. There's no point." Zeyde waited. "Get it? No point? Pencil?"

Abby stopped crocheting. "Your jokes are getting worse, Zeyde."

Bubbe Marcia laughed. "She's a smart kid, that one."

"Eh!" Zeyde waved a hand. "Everybody's a critic. I'll stop telling jokes if you tell me how school's going and if there's anyone special you like in your classes."

"Zeyde!" Abby felt her cheeks redden because she immediately thought of Conrad, who unfortunately wasn't in any of her classes.

Bubbe Marcia nudged him. "You're too nosy, Jordan."

"What? A zeyde shouldn't care about his granddaughter?"

"A zeyde should mind his own business." Bubbe sat up straighter.

Mama Dee came into the living room, wearing an apron over her nice clothes, sweat beading on her forehead. "Dinner's almost ready."

Bubbe Marcia looked concerned. "Where are Rach and Paul? So late? I can't believe the only day they could get an appointment with that specialist was on Rosh Hashanah. It's a *shanda*."

"Soonest appointment Rach could get for him." Mama Dee sat heavily on the couch and fanned herself with her hand. "Rachel texted and said they haven't even been called into the office yet. She wants us to start eating without them."

"Oh, I'd hate to do that," Bubbe Marcia said. "We can wait."

"Speak for yourself," Zeyde Jordan said. "This old goat is hungry. Let's eat!"

Bubbe glared at him, and he zipped it.

Abby crocheted and worried, worried and crocheted. *What's taking them so long? Mom Rachel never does anything on Rosh Hashanah that doesn't have to do with the holiday, so whatever's going on with Paul has to be really serious.*

After another ten minutes and Zeyde's stomach letting out a loud growl, Bubbe said, "Maybe we can get started and have some soup." She patted Zeyde's knee and stood with a groan.

"First," Mama Dee said, "you have to feast your eyes on the desserts."

She led everyone into the kitchen, where the apple cake, rugelach, and challah bread pudding sat on the counter. Their sweet smells mingled with the onion and dill scent coming from the soup bubbling in a pot on the stove.

Zeyde patted his stomach. "Forget the soup. Let's go right to dessert."

Mama Dee smiled.

Bubbe Marcia steered him to his place at the table. "I wish Jeanne and Steve and the kids could be here."

Abby wished that, too. Her Aunt Jeanne and Uncle Steve—Mom Rachel's brother—and her cousins Jared, Elyssa, and Cara came to their house every other Rosh Hashanah. This year, they were celebrating at Aunt Jeanne's sister's house.

On the years her extended family came, they set up an extra table in the living room, and Abby lit the candles with Elyssa and Cara. But today, Abby lit the candles by herself and said the blessing.

"Baruch atah, Adonai Eloheinu, Melech ha-olam asher kide-shanu bemitzvotav vetzivanu lehadlik ner shel Yom Hazikaron.

"Blessed are You, L-rd our G-d, King of the universe, who has sanctified us with Your commandments and has commanded us to light the candle of the Day of Remembrance."

Zeyde poured dark purple wine into the adults' fancy crystal glasses. Abby got grape juice, which she thought was ridiculous. She was twelve now, and a tiny bit of wine wouldn't hurt her. Plus she thought it would be fun to see how it made her feel.

Mama Dee brought out a wicker basket and lifted a cloth napkin to reveal a raisin challah.

"Oooh, that's a beautiful challah, Dee," Bubbe Marcia said.

Mama Dee beamed.

Abby thought about how delicious it was to eat Mama Dee's challah on Rosh Hashanah rather than boring matzo on Passover. Rosh Hashanah was Abby's second-favorite Jewish holiday. Hanukkah was her first. Halloween was her favorite nonreligious holiday.

Zeyde ripped off a piece of the bread and dipped it into a small bowl of agave nectar to symbolize a sweet new year. Mom Rachel switched from honey to agave nectar after she saw a video about how some bees were crushed during the harvesting of honey.

Then Zeyde said the prayer over the bread.

"Baruch atah, Adonai Eloheinu, Melech ha-olam, haMotzi lechem min ha-aretz. Blessed are You, Adonai our G-d, Sovereign of all, who brings forth bread from the earth."

Abby got a funny feeling in her stomach when Mama Dee brought out the bowls of matzo ball soup and her mom and brother *still* weren't home.

"These matzo balls are delish!" Bubbe Marcia declared.

Abby sat a little straighter, as though she'd made them, not just rolled them.

Everyone was spooning up the last of the soup from their bowls when the key turned in the lock and the front door swung open.

Zeyde raised his arms. "Hooray! They're here!"

Bubbe Marcia put a gentle hand on his shoulder, and he quieted.

Mama Dee's whole body tensed.

Mom Rachel walked in first, her face a blank slate.

Abby swallowed a bite of cooked carrot from the soup. It felt like a rock going down her throat.

Paul strode past his mom, stood in front of everyone, and put his palms flat on the table. "Happy New Year, everyone! I have cancer!"

Then he walked to his bedroom and slammed the door.

Everyone turned to Mom Rachel.

She stood, shaking her head, a hand over her mouth.

Mama Dee nearly knocked her chair over, getting up to guide Mom Rachel to the couch.

Bubbe Marcia hurried over and sat on the other side of Mom Rachel, pressed against her, an arm wrapped around her shoulders.

Mom Rachel kept shaking her head. "I can't believe . . . I thought maybe . . . I hoped . . ."

Abby turned to her grandfather.

His head was down, a hand over his eyes, and his shoulders bobbed as he sobbed.

That scared Abby most of all. She'd never seen her zeyde cry.

Slipping away from the table, from the adults, Abby quietly knocked on Paul's door. "Paul?"

He didn't answer, but she pushed his door open anyway.

Paul sat slumped at his desk chair with his back to her.

Abby stood in the doorway, trembling.

Paul turned around. "Come in, Six-Pack."

Abby walked a couple steps closer.

"You can come all the way in. It's not contagious."

Abby sat at the edge of Paul's bed, facing him. Her hands

were balled into fists of determination. "Tell me everything."

Paul let out a breath. "Good news or bad news?"

"All the news, please."

Paul stretched his arms over his head. "Oh, man, this has been such a lousy day."

Abby bit her bottom lip. "I'm sorry."

He shrugged. "Not your fault. Here goes. Bad news first. Turns out I have cancer. The second night of camp, I found a lump on my testicle. When it didn't go away, I googled what it could be and scared myself. Knew I had to tell the moms when I got home."

Abby nodded.

"Ready for the good news part?"

"Mm-hmm."

Paul moved his chair a bit closer. "The urologist said it's a really curable kind of cancer."

Abby bit her thumbnail. "That's good. Right?"

Paul leaned back. "Yeah, it's good, Six-Pack. But I'll need surgery."

"Oh."

"And the urologist consulted with an oncologist."

Abby tilted her head.

"Cancer doctor."

Abby nodded.

"Turns out, I'll need a combination of chemotherapies that will keep me in the hospital a week at a time for each of *four* treatments."

Abby wrinkled her nose. She didn't want her brother in

the hospital. The last time Abby was in a hospital was after her bubbe had a fall, and she visited with Mom Rachel. Abby remembered how bad the hospital smelled—like overcooked cabbage, cleaning fluids, and pee—and how she couldn't wait till they left. "What is that word you said?"

"Chemotherapy?"

"Yes." Abby twisted her hair around a finger.

"It's a medicine that's supposed to kill cancer cells, but it will make me really sick because it attacks healthy cells too. Or at least that's what I think the urologist said. I kind of tuned out after he said the word 'cancer.'"

Abby thought hard for a few moments. "What if you don't get surgery . . . or chemotherapy? What if you don't do anything?"

"Then the cancer will grow. And spread. And I'll die."

"Paul!"

"What? It's true. The sooner they get this out of me, the better. I kind of wish I could have the surgery tomorrow instead of waiting two weeks." He squirmed in his chair.

Abby looked at her brother and knew he didn't deserve this. "I'm really sorry."

"You're sweet, Abs. You know that?"

She didn't know. Abby knew she was sensitive. Mom Rachel told her that. And the kids at school told her she was quiet and antisocial. It was nice her brother thought she was sweet. "Paul?"

"Yeah?" He picked at a splinter of wood at the edge of his desk.

"Are you . . . scared?"

He looked right at her. "What do you think?"

Dumb question. "Yeah. I'd be scared."

"I'm totally freaked—"

The bedroom door opened.

Abby looked up, expecting to see the moms and her grandparents.

Ethan walked in, a baseball cap in his hand. He sat next to Abby on the bed. "Hey, Abs."

"Hey." She wished Ethan hadn't interrupted their conversation. Abby had more questions for her brother.

Ethan squeezed the cap in his hands, like he was wringing out a wet washcloth. "I came as soon as I got your text. I'm so . . . sorry, man."

Paul nodded.

"This sucks," Ethan said.

"Totally," Paul agreed. "Hey, you know where Jake is? He never answered my text."

Ethan was quiet, looking up at Paul and then back at his lap. "Said he had homework or something."

Paul leaned back. "Seriously? Homework? That's . . . whatever."

"I'm going back out there," Abby said, because she realized Ethan might have questions for Paul too, and she should leave them alone.

Paul looked up as Abby walked out. "Hey!"

She turned back.

He touched his palm to his heart. "Love you, Six-Pack."

Abby wanted to say she loved him too, but knew she'd cry

if she opened her mouth. So she nodded and quietly scooted out and shut the door behind her.

Mom Rachel was right.

She was too sensitive.

A little while later, Paul, Ethan, Abby, Bubbe, Zeyde, and the moms crowded around the table in the dining room.

Mama Dee put a piece of each dessert on every person's plate. "This situation calls for desserts," she said. "Lots of desserts."

No one argued.

Everyone ate without talking—there was only the sound of forks clinking against plates and teeth—until Bubbe Marcia looked up and said, "These are absolutely delicious, Dee." But she immediately started crying and excused herself to rush off to the bathroom.

Mom Rachel reached over and squeezed Paul's hand.

He pushed his plate away. "Not hungry."

Ethan stood. "I'd better get home."

Everyone got up from the table, and Bubbe returned from the bathroom, wiping her nose with a long length of toilet paper.

Ethan hugged the moms. "Thanks for having me."

Mama Dee held him an extra few moments. "Thank you for coming over. It means a lot to Paul."

"To all of us," Mom Rachel said.

"Bye, Abs." Ethan waved.

Abby waved back as Ethan hugged Paul and then left.

Mom Rachel scooped Miss Lucy into her arms and kissed

her three times on the head. "It'll be okay," she said to the dog. "Our boy will be okay."

Then Zeyde Jordan hugged Paul and pounded him on the back. "You're gonna beat this."

"I know, Zeyde," Paul said.

Zeyde wiped away tears and stuffed a twenty-dollar bill into Paul's hand.

"Thanks, Zeyde."

Bubbe Marcia held on to Paul extra long. "We love you, Paulie."

"Love you too, Bubbe."

"We'll see you next week for Yom Kippur," Bubbe said. "You tell us if we can do anything before then."

"Will do," Mama Dee said, her lips pressed together, like she was holding back a river of emotions.

After the grandparents left, Paul, Abby, Mom Rachel, and Mama Dee returned to the table, but no one touched their plates.

No one spoke.

Paul's bad news hung in the air like a heavy rain cloud, about to burst open onto all of them.

Finally, Mom Rachel looked up. Her eyes were red-rimmed. "We're going to get through this like we get through everything."

"With food?" Paul asked.

Mama Dee laughed and covered her mouth.

"Together," Mom Rachel said. "We'll get through this together."

"Absolutely." Mama Dee wiped her nose with a napkin.

"All for one and one for . . . well, you know the rest."

The four of them held hands around the table, squeezed tight, and closed their eyes.

If the power of those silent prayers around that table could have healed Paul, he would've walked away that evening cancer-free.

But Paul would need more than prayer to slay this particular beast.

After they cleaned up and everyone went to their rooms, Abby pulled out her journal and captured her thoughts in a poem.

A New Year

The Jewish New Year
Should be a time of celebration
Of starting over, of blessings.
It should be the beginning of a sweet new
year.
It should not be a time of news so bad, so sad
That even three kinds of dessert can't fix it.
This was the worst way
To begin a new year.
Shana tovah, my foot!

Abby put her journal away and turned out the light. "Happy New Year, Fudge."

Her turtle, perched on a rock, did not respond.

How to Atone for Your Sins

Ever since she was eight, Abby had tried to fast on Yom Kippur, the Jewish High Holy Day—the day to atone for your sins from the past year. And every year Abby gave up by early afternoon when her stomach hurt and she thought she might faint.

This year, Abby decided, would be different.

She was determined to fast the entire time until sundown—even though she knew her stomach would hurt and she'd feel dizzy—because this year it was important that she atone for her sins, including not hanging that mezuzah to protect her family as soon as she got it. Deep inside, Abby knew the purpose of the mezuzah wasn't to protect her family; it was meant as a reminder to create a Jewish household. But she couldn't shake the feeling that not putting it up was a mistake, like her selfishness in hiding it under her bed somehow contributed to Paul's illness. Her logical mind knew she was being silly, but her heart worried she had something to do with her brother getting sick. And if that were the case, maybe there was a way she could help him get better.

Since Abby never went to school on Yom Kippur and Jews weren't supposed to do any work, she spent the day in her room, talking to God. Cat and her mom had always spent Yom Kippur at synagogue, but Abby and her family did their talking to God at home.

If I don't eat a single thing during Yom Kippur or take even a sip of water, please make Paul well and take all the cancer away.

By midday it felt like acid was eating through the lining of Abby's gut, but she refused to give in. She wouldn't break her part of the deal with God, figuring it was the least she could do to help her brother.

Abby waited after everyone else started eating to make absolutely sure she'd allowed enough time, even though her mouth watered from the apple-pear-cranberry tart Mama Dee had made as the first course to break the fast.

"Why aren't you eating?" Paul asked.

I'm trying to save you! Abby took a few sips of water and her first bite of tart after twenty-five hours with nothing to eat or drink.

Sweet and sour flavors exploded in her mouth.

Abby never appreciated food so much.

She hoped her small sacrifice of fasting had helped her brother, but she knew there was one more thing she needed to do.

0 0 0

Friday morning before school, Abby reached under her bed and took out the mezuzah Cat had sent her from Israel for her birthday. She ran three fingers over the smooth surface and kissed her fingertips.

Then Abby went into the garage to find a tape measure, a hammer, and two nails.

She measured one third from the top of the doorframe at the entrance to their house and made a tiny mark with a pencil, then said the blessing over the mezuzah.

"*Baruch atah, Adonai Eloheinu, Melech ha-olam, asher kideshanu bemitzvotav vetzivanu likboah mezuzah.*

"Praise to You, Adonai our G-d, Sovereign of the universe, who hallows us with *mitzvot*, commanding us to affix the mezuzah."

Abby checked the measurements three times to be sure it was in the right place, then tilted the mezuzah on the doorframe and started hammering.

She stood back and admired how nice it looked. "There. Should have done that the day I got it."

Conrad came over while she was admiring her work. "Hey, Abs."

Hearing his voice still sent small shivers along Abby's spine. "Oh, hi."

"What's that?" He pointed to the mezuzah.

As they walked to school, Abby explained the significance of the mezuzah. She didn't mention to Conrad that part of the reason she'd hung it was to ward off any more bad things from happening to her family because she knew that was ridiculous. She didn't tell him she worried she might somehow be responsible for what was going on with Paul for the same reason. She didn't mention what was happening with Paul at all.

She hadn't told anyone other than Fudge and Cat.

Fudge, of course, ignored her, as was his way, but when Abby told Cat over video chat, she burst out crying, which proved to Abby that even 6,584.2 miles couldn't keep Cat from being her best friend.

Feeling Your Feelings

A few days later, on Sunday, the night before Paul's surgery—which was called an orchiectomy; Abby had looked it up—he'd planned a going-away party . . . for his testicle.

That morning, Abby video chatted with Cat. "Can you believe he's planning a going-away party? For. His. Testicle?"

Cat burst out laughing. "That's hilarious, Abs."

Abby couldn't believe Cat laughed. When she'd told her that Paul had cancer, Cat had cried. Big tears of deep understanding. Now Cat was laughing. "It's not funny."

Cat curled the bottom of her braid around her finger. "Actually, Abs, it kind of is if you think about it."

Abby had thought about it. It was all she could think about. She didn't understand why her moms were in on this party. It was the day before Paul's surgery. Something could go wrong. Surgery was serious business. Her brother could even die.

When Cat said she had to go meet friends for pizza, Abby was glad to hang up. She was also a little envious that Cat already had new friends, but she didn't. Unless you counted Conrad. He and Abby walked to and from school together, and she'd been to his house, so Abby decided he counted as a new friend. She wouldn't mind having at least one more friend at school, though. It would be nice to have someone to walk to classes with and eat lunch with in the cafeteria, since Conrad had a different lunch period than she did. Abby didn't require a big group to feel comfortable; just one or two good friends was all she needed.

She couldn't think about her lack of friends at the moment, though, because she was filled with worry about Paul's surgery and irritation that they were throwing a party for it.

Abby turned to Fudge's tank. "Why doesn't anyone understand you don't celebrate having cancer?"

Fudge opened his mouth, like he, too, was laughing.

"Et tu, Brute?" Abby collapsed facedown onto her bed, feeling the scratchy yarn from the afghan her bubbe had made for her.

It took every ounce of energy she had to drag herself off the bed and into the living room with her family.

Mom Rachel and Mama Dee were wearing pointy cardboard hats like the ones little kids put on at birthday parties. They even added a sparkly new collar to Miss Lucy with the words PARTY, PARTY, PARTY, so she could be a party girl, too.

Abby stood off to the side of the living room with her arms crossed.

When Mom Rachel approached and tried to put a party hat on Abby's head, she knocked her mom's hand away.

"Hey!" Mom Rachel warned. "Quit being bratty about this, Abigail."

Abby's nostrils flared.

"What is with you today?" Mama Dee searched Abby's face, as though she were looking for answers.

Abby crossed her arms more tightly.

"What's your problem?" Mom Rachel asked.

"I don't have a problem!" Abby exploded. "Maybe I don't think we should be celebrating what's happening to Paul."

Mama Dee stood in front of Abby and put her hands on Abby's shoulders. "We're not celebrating what's happening to your brother. This is what your brother wants. He asked for this, Abs. And it's something we can do for him, so we're doing it."

Abby turned her back to Mama Dee, breaking her mom's grip on her shoulders. "Well, it's stupid. That's all."

Mom Rachel said, "She'll get over herself, Dee. Don't worry."

Abby was about to whirl around and tell Mom Rachel not to talk about her like she wasn't standing right there, but the doorbell rang.

Paul jogged into the living room, wearing socks, shorts, and a T-shirt with a picture of a squirrel carrying an armload of acorns. The T-shirt read, I'M GOING TO KICK TESTICULAR CANCER IN THE NUTS.

Ethan strutted in, carrying a gift.

"Where's Jake?" Paul asked. "Thought he was coming with you."

"Said he'd be here soon," Ethan said.

Ethan dropped his gift on the couch, grabbed Paul into a hug, and pounded him on the back.

Abby was probably the only one who noticed Paul wince from the pounding. Everyone else was too busy getting into party mode.

"Hey there, Miss Abby." Ethan grabbed her into a hug and lifted her off her feet.

Normally, this would make Abby happy, but today she wasn't in the mood.

Abby went to her room, preferring the company of Fudge. He wouldn't be wearing a stupid party hat. He wouldn't be celebrating Paul's upcoming surgery. He would be old, reliable, *boring* Fudge. And that's exactly what Abby needed.

She dove onto her bed and put her pillow over the back of her head, expecting one of the moms to come in and try to convince her to come out and "celebrate" Paul losing his testicle. Abby imagined they'd tell her this wasn't about her and she should be a good sport.

When Abby heard a knock on her bedroom door, she pulled the pillow tighter and didn't answer. As far as she was concerned, the moms could wait out there all night.

The door creaked open. "Six-Pack?"

Abby sat up, turned toward her brother, and clutched the pillow to her chest. "What?" she said in her most annoyed voice, even though she didn't want to be mean to Paul.

"Can I come in?"

"You already are in." She couldn't seem to lose the attitude.

Paul plopped next to Abby on the bed.

"I don't like your shirt," she said. "It's dumb."

"Okay."

"And this party is dumb too. Really dumb!"

Paul put his hand on his sister's knee. "Abs?"

She bit her bottom lip, afraid she'd cry. Abby didn't want to be sad. It was easier to be angry. "What?!"

"Abby," Paul said in his softest voice. "There are two choices here. We can be sad and miserable and tomorrow morning, I'm going to get my nut cut off."

She didn't like Paul talking about it like that.

"Or . . ."

He tipped Abby's chin up so she had to look at him.

She pressed her lips together, determined to stay angry.

"Or . . . we can laugh our butts off tonight, have a great time, and tomorrow morning, I'm going to get my nut cut off."

Abby let out a shaky breath. She hadn't thought about it like that. The bad thing was going to happen to Paul tomorrow morning, whether they laughed or cried tonight. It wouldn't change tomorrow, but everyone might feel a little better tonight. *Maybe*, Abby thought, *that's why Cat laughed. Maybe she understood that it was okay to laugh.* Abby pushed the pillow out of the way and looked at her lap. "I didn't think you could, you know, laugh about cancer. It's really serious."

"It is," Paul admitted. "But you can laugh about almost anything. Just depends on how you approach it."

"I guess that makes sense."

"It totally does, Six-Pack."

"Did Jake ever show up?"

Paul shook his head.

"Why not?" Abby realized she hadn't seen Jake since they'd found out about Paul's cancer. "Is he sick or something?"

Paul shrugged. "Who knows. But will you please come out and join the party? I don't like you hiding in here when we're out there having fun."

Abby nodded.

"Good. We're about to play Pin the Nut on the Squirrel."

"Oh my gosh!" Abby covered her face, then got out of bed. She followed her brother to the living room, where Paul donned one of the pointy party hats.

Abby was the only person not wearing one.

Mom Rachel held one out to her.

Abby grabbed it and broke into a huge grin before putting it on.

"Attagirl!" Paul pumped his fist.

Mom Rachel made everyone fancy limeade spritzers with mint leaves, then Paul opened his presents.

Ethan gave him a cap with a picture of a squirrel holding two acorns.

"For when you lose your hair," he said.

Paul ran a hand through his thick, dark hair. "Yeah, thanks for that."

Ethan punched Paul in the shoulder.

Paul punched him back, then began unwrapping a gift from the moms. "What is it?"

Mama Dee shrugged.

"You should know," Paul said. "You got it."

"No I didn't," Mama Dee replied. "I'll be as surprised as you are. You know Mom Rachel takes care of presents."

We laughed.

Inside the box were a couple dozen acorns.

"Ha ha," Paul said. "Everybody's a comedian." Then he looked a little sad.

"Come on, kid." Mama Dee tapped his shoulder. "Time for a game!"

Abby thought she should have gotten her brother a present, even if she didn't like the idea of a party. She could have bought him a new book of banjo music or a funny cap like Ethan did, or . . . something to show she loved him.

"Game time!" Ethan shouted.

They were in the middle of Pin the Nut on the Squirrel when the doorbell rang.

Paul looked at Ethan. "Jake?"

Ethan shrugged, then looked down.

"I'll get it," Abby said.

When she opened the door, Conrad stood there, wearing shorts, a T-shirt, and flip-flops. "Hey, Abs, I texted you but . . ." He peeked around her.

Abby wondered what Conrad thought about the things he was seeing—people in pointy party hats, a giant poster of a squirrel on the wall with little acorns stuck all over it, and, Abby realized, Paul and Ethan trying to do handstand push-ups against the wall . . . and failing miserably.

Abby yanked off her pointy hat, snapping her chin with the rubber band in the process. It reminded her of the first time she'd met Conrad and was wearing that silly birthday tiara. "You were? Texting me? Sorry. My phone's in my room."

"I wanted to see if you felt like walking into town. I'm kind of bored."

"Let's go outside." Abby grabbed Conrad by the elbow and led him out into the humid night air because she realized it had gotten quiet behind her, which meant everyone was probably staring at them.

Outside on the porch, Abby swatted away a mosquito as Conrad whispered, "Um, what was going on in there?"

"It was . . . well . . ." Abby didn't know how to explain, especially because she hadn't told Conrad what was going on with Paul. She looked at him, opened her mouth, closed it, then burst out crying.

I'm definitely too sensitive!

"Oh wow. Abby, are you . . . ?" Conrad opened his arms, then dropped them at his sides. "Can I . . . ?"

Abby sniffed and nodded.

Conrad moved a step closer, wrapped his arms awkwardly around her, and gently patted Abby's back. "It's okay. Whatever it is, it's okay."

Abby pulled away and stepped back, shaking her head. "It isn't."

Conrad's soft brown eyes held nothing but compassion, so Abby blurted, "My brother has cancer."

His mouth opened.

Abby wished she hadn't said anything. Being quiet felt safer than sharing hard things.

Conrad moved a step closer. And another step.

He didn't say anything, which left room for Abby to talk.

"It's testicular cancer. He's getting surgery . . ." She sniffed hard. "Tomorrow morning. Really early."

Conrad still didn't say anything, so Abby told him the truest thing. "I'm scared."

"Abby, I'm sorry."

She hiccuped and wiped her leaking eyes. "I'm most scared that Paul might . . . that he could . . . die." She hadn't shared that fear with anyone. Abby knew some people did die during surgery. Some people died from testicular cancer. Abby wished desperately that she could go back in time, back before she knew about Paul's cancer, when she thought the worst thing in the world was Cat moving away.

"Abby?"

"Mm-hmm?"

"I need to tell you something. It's important."

Abby nodded to show she was listening.

"My uncle—the one I told you about who's a cook?"

"Yes?"

"He had testicular cancer."

Had? Abby's heart thundered because she assumed

Conrad's uncle must have died. She bit the inside of her cheek and waited for him to say the awful words.

"He had the same surgery your brother is probably getting. And chemo. Lots of chemo. His hair fell out from that. But you know what?"

"What?" Abby's voice trembled.

"He's been doing great ever since. His surgery and chemo happened three years ago. I was ten. He works in a restaurant now. He plays basketball and goes kayaking and runs, like, twenty-five miles a week."

"Your uncle's . . . fine?"

"Yeah, he totally kicks my butt whenever we play basketball even though he's way older than me."

Abby let this new information swirl through her mind. Maybe Paul would be okay. She thought about how good Conrad's uncle must be at basketball because Conrad was good. "Then your uncle could definitely kick *my* butt in basketball."

Conrad laughed. "Abby, a three-year-old could kick your butt in basketball."

"Ouch."

"Sorry."

"A coconut could kick my butt in basketball," Abby said.

Conrad smiled. "A ladybug."

"Now you're just being mean."

They both laughed.

Conrad ran a hand through his hair. "It really could, though."

Abby shoved his shoulder, but she burst out laughing. "It probably could."

Then they both got quiet.

"Hey, I'm sorry about what your brother has to go through. But I really think he'll be okay, you know, when his treatments are over."

Those words made Abby's heart feel lighter. "I hope so. Hey, Conrad?"

"Yeah?"

"Do you want to come in? My brother's having a going-away party . . . for . . . for his . . ." Abby couldn't say the word. "The part of his body that has the cancer."

"I could come in for a while," Conrad said. "If it's all right with your family. I don't want to—"

"It's definitely all right. My moms have a 'the more the merrier' philosophy when it comes to parties."

Abby opened the door, and they walked in. "Everybody," Abby said, "this is my friend Conrad." The word "friend" felt good and right. She was sure now that he was a new friend. "Conrad?" Abby waved her arm. "This is . . . everybody."

"Welcome, Conrad!" Mama Dee offered him a pointy hat.

Mom Rachel shoved a limeade spritzer into his hand.

Abby put her silly hat back on.

Paul handed Conrad a paper acorn with Velcro on it so he could take a turn at Pin the Nut on the Squirrel.

"You'll do great, man." Ethan clapped.

Blindfolded, Conrad was spun around a few too many

times by Mama Dee, and then he tried to pin the acorn on the wall, the couch, and a floor lamp, nearly knocking it over.

Paul grabbed the lamp before it fell.

When Conrad peeled off his blindfold and saw how far he was from the target, everyone cracked up.

He stood close to Abby and whispered, "I guess I play Pin the Nut about as well as you play basketball."

Abby burst out giggling and covered her mouth. She loved that they shared their first inside joke.

When everyone was leaving, Conrad gave Abby another quick hug. "See you tomorrow."

Until that moment, Abby had been angry with her moms for telling her she couldn't go with them to wait during Paul's surgery and that she had to go to school. But now Abby was glad she'd get to walk there with Conrad in the morning and could talk to him if she was feeling nervous. She knew she'd made the right choice telling him about Paul's cancer instead of keeping it bottled up, and Conrad made her feel better by sharing what had happened with his uncle. "See you tomorrow, Conrad."

Abby could still feel the ghost sensations from his hug.

After Conrad left, Paul walked Ethan to the door. "Thanks for coming, Eth." Paul gave his friend a tight hug.

"No worries. I'll come visit tomorrow, after it's, um, over . . . if you want."

Neither of them said anything for a few seconds.

"Yeah, I'll let you know how I'm doing."

"Cool."

After Ethan left, Mom Rachel said, "I like that boy."

"But Jake." Mama Dee shook her head. "Why wasn't he here with you?"

"Something difficult is going on with you," Mom Rachel said, "and he's nowhere to be found?"

Paul shrugged and went to his room.

After Paul walked away, Mom Rachel whispered to Mama Dee, "I sure hope Jake shows up when Paul goes through surgery and treatments. He'll need all the friends and support he can get."

Mama Dee filled her cheeks with air and let it out. She put her arm around Mom Rachel's shoulders and leaned her head down against hers. "We all will."

Abby got a pain in her gut, wishing Cat were still here. *At least there's Conrad*, she thought. Then Abby realized her moms might have been talking about Cat's mom and wishing she were still living next door.

"At least we have Bubbe Marcia and Zeyde Jordan," Abby offered.

Mama Dee pulled Abby into their hug. "And Aunt Jeanne, Uncle Steve, and your cousins."

"We'll be okay," Mom Rachel said, but Abby heard the hesitation in her voice.

Mama Dee looked into Abby's eyes and then into Mom Rachel's, then toward Paul's room. "He'll be okay."

"He will," Mom Rachel agreed. "He has to be."

Thinking about Conrad's uncle, Abby said, "He definitely will."

Abby helped her moms clean up before she retreated to her bedroom, exhausted but surprisingly happy.

"Who knew," she said to Fudge, "the night before Paul's surgery could actually be fun?"

Fudge showed his enthusiasm by not budging from his rock.

Abby couldn't fall asleep; her mind whirled with happy thoughts of Conrad hugging her, mixed with worried thoughts about Paul's surgery. She imagined how much it must hurt to have surgery and how scary it must be for her brother. The longer Abby couldn't fall asleep, the more she thought about the statistics she'd read online. Some people died from testicular cancer. Not many, but some. Paul could be one of those. Just because everyone kept saying he'd be okay didn't mean he actually would.

She got out of bed, checked on Fudge, and then went to the bathroom between Paul's and her bedrooms.

The house was dark and quiet. Abby heard frogs croaking in the canal behind their home. She loved when the house was quiet enough to hear the frogs' nighttime concert. It was the perfect background music for deep thinking.

When Abby came out of the bathroom, she heard a different sound. A wounded noise, like someone might be hurt. At first, Abby thought it could be Miss Lucy with her paw caught in a door or something, but then she wondered if she was imagining the sad sound because she was so sleep-deprived.

Abby's heart squeezed when she realized it was coming from Paul's bedroom. She almost sprinted across the great room to get her moms, but instead she took a couple steps closer to Paul's bedroom door and listened carefully.

Abby heard muffled sobbing and imagined Paul in bed, clutching his pillow to his chest and crying into the darkness.

She wanted to barge in and hug her brother like Conrad had hugged her out on the porch. She wanted to tell Paul about Conrad's uncle and how he'd probably be okay after all the hard parts were over. Mostly, she wanted Paul to know he wasn't alone.

But something kept Abby from opening Paul's door. It wasn't fear. Abby somehow knew Paul needed to be alone with his feelings, even though they were hard and scary. She understood Paul had a right to experience those things without her coming in and trying to keep him from them.

As softly as she could, Abby whispered into the wood of his door, "I love you, Paul Braverman. You're one of the best people I know." She hoped the words traveled from her heart to his.

Then Abby crept back into her bed and pulled the turtle-shell afghan up to her chin, straining to hear her brother's painful sobs in the darkness.

The First Hard Part

The next day, in language arts class, Abby kept tapping her foot. She couldn't wait until the bell rang and she could sneak a peek at her phone. She knew Paul should be done with his surgery by now. Mom Rachel explained that the whole surgery would take no more than an hour. But if Abby looked at her phone during class, her teacher, Ms. Petroccia, might take it, and then Abby wouldn't get it back until the end of the school day. She couldn't let that happen.

"Okay, class." Ms. Petroccia clapped her hands. "Since there are twenty-one of you, we're going to break into seven groups of three to work on our poetry projects."

Abby's heart did a little zing because she loved poetry, but then it sank like a stone because she did *not* like group work. Poetry was quiet and personal. It meant reaching deep inside and pulling out bits of your heart to sprinkle onto the page. It wasn't the stuff of collaboration.

Why do teachers keep shoving us into groups, Abby wondered, *when solo work is so much more satisfying and less stressful?*

By the time Abby gathered her notebook and pen and looked around, everyone had already formed groups. *What if there's no place for me?*

Nearby, Miranda Gross and Laura Fournier had pushed their desks together and were talking. Abby didn't join them. She'd work quietly at her desk and hope Ms. Petroccia didn't notice.

The class was supposed to decide which poetry project they wanted to do from the three choices on the board and brainstorm ideas about that project.

Abby opened her notebook to a fresh page and wrote *Paul.*

Then *surgery.*

Before she could write another word, Ms. Petroccia appeared in front of her desk.

Abby slid her arm over her notebook.

Her teacher tapped Abby's desk with her fingernail. "Go over and join Miranda and Laura. They need a third in their group."

As soon as Ms. Petroccia turned, Abby scribbled out the two words she'd written and picked up her notebook and pen.

She pushed a desk toward the two girls. It made a loud screech, and everyone in the class turned to look at her. Abby slipped into a chair, slunk low, and wished for the millionth time that her moms had let her go to the hospital where Paul was having his surgery, so she could know the minute he was done. Abby had a burning urge to look at her phone, but she forced herself to resist. She couldn't lose her phone. Not today.

Abby turned to a clean page in her notebook and waited for Miranda to take charge, like she usually did.

Miranda pulled her own notebook toward herself, away from Abby's desk. It was a small gesture, but Abby noticed.

"Okay, what should we do for our project?" Miranda pointed to the list on the board. "A small book of poems? A video of several spoken poems? Or a poetry-inspired art project?

"Abby?" Miranda asked in a too-loud voice.

Abby didn't want to respond first because she had a feeling that if she said what she wanted to do—a small book of poems—it would be the exact wrong answer. There was a long pause; Abby sank lower in her chair.

Laura shook her head at Abby to show that not answering was the exact wrong answer. "Well, I think the art project would be the most fun."

"I agree," Miranda said. "Well, what do you think?"

Both girls stared at Abby.

She shrugged. Abby didn't want to do the art project. She didn't want to do any project with Miranda and Laura. All Abby wanted was to hear from her moms. *What if something went wrong during the surgery?*

"You know . . ." Miranda turned to see where Ms. Petroccia was.

Their teacher was seated at her desk, looking over some papers.

Miranda leaned toward Abby. "You should talk more."

"Or at all." Laura laughed, but it wasn't a funny sound.

"I'm only telling you this to help," Miranda said softly. "You know, it's weird when you don't talk."

Then Laura added in a whisper, "That's why no one wants to be your friend, Abby. You seem like a snob."

Abby glanced around the classroom, wondering who else thought she seemed like a snob.

"You really do," Miranda said. "And like I said, we're only telling you to help you be better."

Abby pressed her lips together and breathed hard through her nostrils.

"I mean," Miranda continued, "would you even yell if there was an emergency, like a fire?"

Laura leaned closer and whispered, "Or would you let people die?"

What a terrible thing to say, Abby thought. *How can they talk about people dying? Especially today!* Of course Abby would yell to save someone in an emergency. Wouldn't she?

"You're too weird to be in our group." Laura waved Abby away with a flick of her wrist, like she was a pesky mosquito.

Abby picked up her notebook and pen and moved back to her own desk. She stared at the page in front of her and drew Xs, pressing so hard, she ripped through the paper. When she looked up, Ms. Petroccia was staring at her from her desk at the front of the room. What if Ms.

Petroccia told her she had to go back and sit with Miranda and Laura?

Abby couldn't let that happen. She grabbed her things and rushed to Ms. Petroccia's desk. In the tiniest voice, Abby said, "I need to use the bathroom." She almost said, *It's an emergency*, but that reminded her of the mean things Miranda and Laura had just said to her.

Ms. Petroccia handed Abby a hall pass, and Abby fast-walked down the hall, away from those awful girls. They acted like being quiet was a disease they didn't want to catch. On the way to the bathroom, Abby thought of running out of school and figuring out how to get to the hospital. She could return the dumb hall pass to Ms. Petroccia tomorrow.

Instead, Abby went to the bathroom and locked herself in the first stall. It smelled bad. She held her breath and sorted through what had happened. Tears pricked at the edges of her eyes.

She needed to tell Cat about it. Cat was friendly with Miranda and Laura, but she didn't like the way they talked about other people all the time. Abby would text her, and Cat would probably reply to her right away, telling her to ignore those stupid girls, that she was so much better than they were. That she wasn't a snob, but a quiet, thoughtful person. Abby knew Cat would have her back, even from 6,584.2 miles away.

With trembling hands, Abby pulled out her phone to text her best friend.

She never got a chance to text Cat, though, because there was a message waiting for her from Mom Rachel.

Paul's out of surgery. He did great!

That's when Abby finally let the tears flow.

"Hey, slow down!"

Conrad jogged to catch up to Abby after school.

"I have to get home," she called behind her.

"Oh, that's right." Conrad reached her. "Your brother's surgery was today."

"My mom told me he did okay, but I want to get home and see him."

The two of them jogged all the way to their houses, their backpacks knocking on their spines the whole time.

"Tell your brother I hope he's doing okay," Conrad said, but Abby was already jamming her key into the lock.

When she saw her brother lying on the couch, Abby let out a breath she hadn't realized she'd been holding.

Paul's head lay on a pillow from his bed, and a package of frozen petite peas—Mom Rachel's version of an ice pack—rested on his lower stomach.

Abby dropped her backpack and plopped onto the floor next to Paul. "How are you? How was it?"

He blinked at her and smiled. "Six-Pack!"

Paul was happy to see her. It almost, *almost* made up for the mean things Miranda and Laura had said about her in language arts class. *How can people be so unkind?*

"I'm still sort of . . ."

Mom Rachel walked into the living room, wiping her hands on a towel. "He's still out of it, Abs. The anesthesia's working its way through his system."

"I'm good . . . Six-Pack," Paul slurred. Then he licked his lips, and Mom Rachel went back into the kitchen and got him a glass of water to sip on with a straw.

"Let me grab your pain medicine," Mom Rachel said.

Paul sat up, swallowed two pills with a grimace and a swig of water, and then lay back down. "What?"

"I'm just looking at you," Abby said.

"Stop worrying. I'm okay."

"You know you have a bag of frozen petite peas on you, right?" Abby grinned.

Paul laughed, then winced. "Ow. Laughing hurts."

"Sorry." Abby told herself to be as unfunny as possible while Paul recuperated.

"It's okay," Paul said softly. "It only hurts when I laugh. Or cough. Or walk. Or breathe."

"Really?"

Paul licked his lips again. "Breathing doesn't hurt."

"Hey," Abby said, "maybe when you feel better, we can play Monopoly to, you know, take your mind off things."

"That would be gravy."

"Gravy?" Abby asked.

But when she looked at Paul, his eyelids were closed and he was breathing softly through slightly parted lips.

"Gravy." Abby shook her head, then tiptoed away and sat on a stool at the counter so she could talk with Mom Rachel. "Paul *is* out of it! He said 'gravy' instead of 'great.'"

Mom Rachel laughed. "Maybe he's hungry."

Abby studied her mom. "Did everything really go well today? Is there anything you're not telling me? Paul's acting weird."

Mom Rachel put a glass of seltzer in front of Abby. "Honey, that's how it is after surgery. You're out of it and you sleep a lot. The surgeon said there were no complications and Paul did great."

Abby took a bubbly sip of seltzer. "I'm glad he's okay. I was worried today in school." She decided not to tell her mom about Miranda and Laura since she had enough to think about with Paul. "What's next?"

Mom Rachel leaned on the counter. "They'll test the tumor and let us know the best treatment, although they already gave us a good idea of what it will be. It's going to be tough."

Abby nodded.

"We'll have to help Paul get through it."

Feeling like a knight on a horse about to ride in and save the day, Abby said, "We've got this, Mom."

"Love you, Abs."

Abby let her mom's words fill her up.

"I should be making a new YouTube video for my channel today, but . . ." Mom Rachel tilted her head toward the living room where Paul was asleep on the couch. "If I don't put the videos out on a weekly schedule, my subscribers tend to drop off. Then I don't make as much money from advertisers. Or from my e-cookbook sales."

"Maybe you could make the video tomorrow."

Mom Rachel nodded. "Guess I'll be making that one solo. Paul will probably spend the day in bed tomorrow."

Abby thought about helping her mom with the video, and her stomach bunched into a knot. "I guess so."

"Want a snack, Abs?"

She shook her head. "I'm going to sit out there with Paul."

"He might keep sleeping. We can't expect much from him today."

"That's all right." Abby finished her seltzer. "I just want to be near him."

Mom Rachel reached out and patted Abby's hand. "You're a good sister. You know that?"

Abby nodded. *Paul is a good brother.* She went into her room and grabbed her supplies to work on crocheting her endless afghan in the living room near Paul. Sitting on the chair near him, Abby kept an eye on him while she crocheted.

Mom Rachel came into the living room, removed the frozen petite peas ice pack, and tossed it into the freezer. She brought it back twenty minutes later. "To keep the swelling down," she whispered to Abby.

Later, Mama Dee came home from her shop, Dee's Delights, with a box of Paul's favorite cupcakes—chocolate ganache with peanut butter frosting.

Everyone took care of Paul in the best way they knew how.

Even Miss Lucy curled up at the end of the couch by Paul's feet and napped with him.

Abby felt sure Fudge was sending Paul good turtle-y thoughts from his tank in her bedroom.

When Abby and Conrad got home from school the next day, Paul was sitting on a folding chair in front of the garage.

"Hey, Six-Pack!" He waved, then hunched forward.

Abby ran over and gave her brother a quick hug. "How are you doing?"

"Hey, man." Conrad shook Paul's hand. "Hope you're feeling okay."

"I'm good," Paul said. "Thanks."

Conrad nodded. "Well, I'll see you later. Tons of homework."

Abby waved, then after Conrad went into his house/Cat's house, she got a folding chair from the garage and sat next to her brother. It felt good to sit outside with him in the warm sunshine.

"Glad you're home," Paul said. "It's boring sitting around all day while everyone else is in school. I couldn't even play the banjo. It hurt to hold it on my lap."

"Ow. Sorry." Abby patted her brother's arm. "Where's Mom Rachel?"

"Food shopping."

Abby leaned forward. "Can I get you anything?"

"Like frozen petite peas?"

Abby grinned. "One time I had to wear frozen petite peas

on my head like a hat after I stood up really fast and banged it on the underside of a drawer."

"Oh, I remember that. You looked ridiculous walking around with frozen petite peas on your head. The moms have to buy an actual ice pack."

"They really do." Abby pulled her legs up and wrapped her arms around her knees. "You seem so much better today." Abby wanted to believe this meant Paul would be fine and maybe not even need chemotherapy.

"Yeah, I guess I was out of it yesterday from the anesthesia. I'm still sore, though." Paul shifted in his chair and grimaced. "It hurts to walk. And sit. And move."

"Anything I can do to help?"

Paul shook his head. "Nah, it should get better soon, but I want to go back to school. It's boring at home. Mom Rachel said I have to give it at least one more day. She doesn't want anyone bumping into me in the halls."

"Yeah, I guess that would hurt."

"It would, but if I could leave class—"

Mom Rachel pulled her car into the driveway. She smiled and waved through the windshield.

"Paul, I'm really glad the surgery is over."

"Me too. Wish I was all done with the chemo, too."

Abby saw worry in her brother's eyes.

"Groceries!" Mom Rachel called after she opened the car door.

Paul and Abby got up and met Mom Rachel at the trunk of her car.

Mom Rachel poked Paul in the chest. "Not you, buddy. No lifting yet. Abby and I have got this."

Abby smiled at her mom's confidence in her and carried four bags at once while her mom carried two.

"Show-off," Paul teased Abby.

She did bicep curls with the heavy bags and watched Paul walk haltingly into the house.

"I'm exhausted watching you both carry all those bags," Paul said. "I'm going to take a quick nap."

Mom Rachel kissed him on the cheek. "Rest well, sweetheart. Dinner will be ready when you get up."

"Thanks, Mom."

Miss Lucy pranced behind Paul and followed him into his room.

"I think that dog is your brother's number one caretaker. She's been his little shadow since Paul got home from surgery."

"The whole family has Paul's back," Abby said.

Mom Rachel smiled. "It seems that way."

Abby helped her mom put away groceries, but the minute she set up the camera to start filming, Abby hurried to her room and sat on her desk chair. "I'm not feeling brave enough to help Mom with her videos yet," she told Fudge.

Fudge settled onto his rock and looked at Abby with his mouth open.

Even though Miranda and Laura had ignored Abby since they offered her their unwanted "advice," their words still rattled around in her brain, making her doubt herself.

"Those girls are mean," she told Fudge, "but they're not wrong."

Abby put her head in her hands. "I'll probably never make a friend in my classes. No one will ever want to eat lunch with me. I don't even know why Conrad wants to be my friend. He'll probably dump me as soon as he finds someone better."

Fudge opened his mouth wider, like he was paying attention.

Abby let out a sigh.

He slipped into the water and swam to Abby so their faces were only centimeters apart with the glass of the tank between them.

"Thanks, buddy." Abby touched her fingers to the tank. "You're a good listener."

Just about three weeks after his surgery, Paul felt well enough to take Abby to her favorite place—Winding River Park.

As soon as they got out of the car, a peacock with its feathers fanned out approached. When it let out a sharp squawk, Abby shrieked.

Paul put a hand on her shoulder. "It's okay, Abs."

"They're so loud." Abby caught her breath. "And unexpected."

"The world is loud and unexpected," Paul said.

As they walked toward the entrance of the park, Abby thought about what Paul said. Loud cars. Loud TV. Loud people, like Miranda and Laura. The park was different, though. There were sounds, but peaceful ones—a squirrel running up a tree, a deer bounding through the woods, a breeze rustling palm fronds. The quiet of the woods always restored Abby in a way that helped her deal with the loud world outside the park.

Paul and Abby walked side by side through the canopy of trees at the entrance and over a wooden bridge, their sneakers tapping on the planks.

Abby breathed in the smell of fresh pine, and also decaying leaves. "I love it here."

"I know you do, Six-Pack."

"You sure this isn't too much walking for you?"

"Nah," Paul said. "I feel really good now."

Abby wrapped an arm around her brother's skinny waist, leaned into him, and squeezed. "I wish you didn't have to start chemotherapy tomorrow."

"Let's not talk about it."

Abby nodded.

They walked along the sandy path, paying careful attention to the trees they passed in case they spotted a baby owl. That had happened only once, and Paul was the one who had noticed it. He had pointed Abby toward the hole in a tree where an owl was perched. She had felt tingles as she looked at the little owl, who was more feathers than anything else. Abby had hoped to spot another owl ever since, but with no luck so far.

As they curved around the path that ran along the water, Abby pointed at three turtles sunning on a log in the shallow, slow-moving wisp of an offshoot of the river. "Look. Fudge's cousins."

"Ha. Yeah. Oh, Abs, look past the turtles." Paul positioned Abby so she had a clear view of the far bank of the river where a gator was sunning itself.

"Cool."

"Yeah, I'm glad it's on that side, though."

"Me too."

After they passed a small orange grove and continued along the shaded path, a pack of wild turkeys gobbled after one another and ran across the path to the other side of the woods, which made Paul and Abby laugh so hard, they stopped and bent over.

"Turkeys are hilarious," Paul said.

"They really are."

Abby noticed Paul didn't wince from laughing or bending. He was doing so much better since his surgery that it was hard for Abby to believe he could still have something as scary as cancer inside his body, but Mama Dee explained that even though the surgeon removed his diseased testicle, there could still be cancer cells in Paul's body. That's why he needed chemotherapy to get rid of all of them.

Abby wished she could stay in the park like this forever. No cancer treatments. No lonely lunchroom in her crowded middle school. No Miranda and Laura. But staying in the park forever would also mean no more walking to and from school with Conrad, and that wouldn't be worth it.

Paul and Abby continued to the back of the park, not

talking, just noticing. Then they strolled around the big tree-lined loop that would eventually lead them to the trail out.

Abby squinted at bright sunlight filtering through the leaves. "I don't want this walk to end."

Paul stopped and looked up too. "Yeah. I'm not looking forward to tomorrow. I have no idea what to expect, other than it's going to make me really sick before it makes me better."

Abby reached for her brother's hand. "Paul, please be okay."

He squeezed his sister's fingers. "I'll do my best, Six-Pack."

Round One

Abby woke before her alarm the next morning and dressed quickly, yanking on jeans, a T-shirt, and her black Converse. Her sneakers weren't colorful like Mom Rachel's rainbow ones, but she loved them anyway.

She still couldn't believe her moms were letting her go to the hospital to help Paul get settled in for his week of chemotherapy. Abby didn't want to do anything that might make them change their minds, like not being ready on time. She knew if they made her go to school, she'd spend the whole time worrying about Paul and wouldn't be able to focus on her work anyway.

"Come on, Paul," Mama Dee said from the hallway outside Abby's bedroom door. "There's no way around this, bud. You have to go."

Abby stood very still but couldn't hear what Paul said. *What if Paul refuses to go to the hospital? What if there is cancer in his body and it keeps growing? He promised he'd do his best to be okay.*

Abby opened her door, not sure what she could do to help convince her brother to go to the hospital and get his treatment.

Paul, with his hair sticking up in forty-two different directions, shuffled in front of her and went into the bathroom as though it were any other day.

Mama Dee, hand on her hip, nodded.

Abby let out a breath, then prepared food for Fudge—carrots, green beans, and bok choy. Once her turtle was happily munching on his veggies, Abby packed a bag of things to do in the hospital in case there would be a lot of waiting. She brought the notebook from Cat if she felt inspired to write a poem, and a book of Mary Oliver's poetry, which her Aunt Jeanne and Uncle Steve had given her last Hanukkah. Sometimes Mary Oliver's poems transported her to Winding River Park and filled her with peace. Abby also added a deck of cards if Paul got bored and wanted to play a game with her or play Solitaire when he was by himself.

"Hey, Butterbean," Mom Rachel said when Abby came out to the kitchen.

Abby noticed dark circles under her mom's eyes.

"Hey, Mom."

Mama Dee filled a coffee mug, then picked up her phone and started tapping keys. "Want to make sure they remember the big cupcake order we got yesterday. And that fire truck birthday cake is going to be picked up this morning."

Mom Rachel reached an arm around Mama Dee. "They'll remember everything, hon."

Mama Dee put down her phone. "I know. I'm just nervous."

Mom Rachel nodded. "We all are."

Miss Lucy barked.

"Oh, I almost forgot to feed her. My head's a mess today." Mom Rachel filled Miss Lucy's bowl and put it on the floor as Paul came out.

"Guess I'm ready," he said.

Mom Rachel gave him a hug and leaned her cheek on his chest.

Mama Dee held up her mug. "Coffee, Paul?"

"Nah." Paul came over and rested his chin on top of Abby's head. "Ew. Six-Pack, you need to wash your hair."

"Paul!"

"What? You do."

Abby wasn't really mad at him, and she couldn't remember the last time she had washed her hair. "I'll wash it tonight."

"Good." Paul held his nose. "P. U."

"Paul!" Abby was secretly glad her brother was able to goof around a little on the morning he would start chemotherapy.

Mama Dee put her mug in the sink. "I hate to say this, but we'd better get going."

Paul swallowed. "Guess so."

Abby ran up and hugged him tight.

He patted her back. "It'll be okay, Six-Pack."

But it sounded to Abby like Paul was saying the words to convince himself. He wasn't doing a good job of it; Abby noticed him shivering, and it wasn't cold in the house.

On the drive to the hospital, Paul looked out his window in the back seat and didn't talk.

Abby thought about reaching over and patting his knee, but when she looked closely, she saw her brother nervously tapping his fingers. This made *her* nervous.

She pulled out her phone and texted Cat.

> **Paul is the bravest person I know. We're heading to the hospital right now for his first chemotherapy treatment. He didn't want to go, but we're going.**

Cat responded immediately.

> **You're brave too, Abby. Wish I could be there for you. xoxo**

Abby hadn't thought of herself as brave. Cat always saw things in her that she didn't see in herself. Her phone vibrated. Abby thought it was another message from Cat, but it was from Conrad.

> **I'll miss walking to school with you today. Hope everything goes okay with your brother.**

Abby closed her eyes for a moment. She didn't have Cat

to help her through this, but Conrad was proving to be a supportive friend.

She replied to his text.

> **We're almost at the hospital now. Mama Dee will bring me to school as soon as Paul settles in, so we can walk home together.**

Sounds good. See you soon, Abby.

Conrad's text made Abby feel better. It was good to know she'd have the walk home from school to look forward to.

As they pulled into the hospital parking lot, Abby put her phone away and glanced at her brother.

Paul looked like he might throw up, and he hadn't even gotten any chemo yet.

Mama Dee swiveled around from the passenger seat and tapped Paul's knee. "You ready for this, bud?"

He shook his head. "I'm scared because I have no idea what to expect."

Mom Rachel pulled into a spot and cut the engine. She reached her hand back, and Paul grabbed it.

"We're here for you, Paul," Mom Rachel said.

Mama Dee put her hand on top. "We've all got your back."

Abby put her hand on top of theirs.

Paul inhaled deeply and then exhaled. "Okay. Let's do this thing."

Bravest person I know, Abby thought.

0 0 0

Abby stayed close to her family as they walked through the doors into the hospital.

Everything was painted in bright colors—oranges, reds, and purples—and there were big pictures of monkeys hanging from the ceiling over the counter where someone said, "Good morning. May I help you?"

Looking at the child-friendly decorations, Paul muttered, "Great."

Mama Dee poked him and smiled for the woman at the counter. "Yes, we need to check him in for the fifth floor."

"Oncology," the woman said. "May I see your ID and have the name of the patient?"

"Paul Braverman," Mama Dee said while she pulled out her license.

The woman made a call, then said, "They're all ready for you upstairs, Paul. The elevators are around that corner."

Everyone but Paul had to get their photo taken and was handed a visitor's badge to wear.

When the elevator door opened on the fifth floor, Abby saw more bright colors and a circular desk, with people in medical scrubs and lots of computers and other machines. It smelled clean, with an underlying whiff of medicine.

As they walked to the desk, Abby peeked into one of the patient's rooms and immediately wished she hadn't. There was a lump curled under a white sheet. The lump was hooked up to some kind of machine that had a plastic bag of fluid hanging from it. The lump—pale and frail—barely looked like a person.

Abby turned away from the sight, hoping her brother didn't end up looking like that.

"Welcome, Paul," said a woman with tight blond curls and blue scrubs with baby elephants on them. "I'm Nicole. I'll be your nurse today. Let's get you settled into your room."

She must've noticed Paul staring at her scrubs. "Oh, don't mind these," she said. "Most of my patients are younger than you."

There were a lot of little kids in beds in the rooms they passed.

"Is this floor supposed to be only for little kids?" Paul asked Nurse Nicole.

"Oh no. We just have a lot of little ones on the floor right now, but it's also for teenagers like you."

Abby looked into another room they passed, and a bald boy was lying in bed, watching TV. Her stomach tightened, thinking about what Paul would look like bald. Her brother had such nice, thick hair. Maybe it wouldn't fall out. Maybe Paul would get through treatments without many side effects.

"We have an awesome teen lounge at the end of the hall," Nurse Nicole said. "It's got video games, a library, a table to play games, and a music station with instruments, like guitars, a keyboard, and a banjo."

Paul and the moms looked at one another.

Abby gave Paul a discreet fist bump, as though having a banjo in the teen lounge would make up for Paul having to be hospitalized.

Everything in Paul's room was white. White sheets. White walls. But there were decorations, too. A painting of a person holding a couple dozen colorful balloons. It looked like he was floating. There was a TV hanging near the ceiling and a bathroom and a window that looked out onto the parking lot.

"This is it," Nurse Nicole said. "Did you bring your own pajamas, Paul?"

He shook his head.

Nurse Nicole went into the closet and pulled out a blue gown. "You can go into the bathroom and put this on, but you're welcome to bring your own pajamas. That's what most of the kids do. Makes them feel more comfortable."

Abby had a feeling Mom Rachel would be buying Paul funny pajamas to cheer him up.

"Get settled," Nurse Nicole said. "I'll be back to put on your medical bracelet and hook you up so we can get some fluids in you. And please don't hesitate to ask me anything. I'm probably more accurate than Google, and I'll bring you ice cream if you play your cards right."

Abby remembered the playing cards she had brought and put them on the table near Paul's bed.

"Thanks, Six-Pack," Paul said, and then he went into the bathroom to change.

"Not so bad." Mama Dee looked around the room.

"I guess," Mom Rachel said. "There are a lot of little kids here. It's sad."

"So sad." Mama Dee smoothed the white blanket on

Paul's bed. "Maybe I could bring some cupcakes for them, if the nurses say it's okay."

Mom Rachel grabbed Mama Dee's hand and leaned her head on her shoulder. "That would be nice, babe. The exploding unicorn ones."

"Of course."

"And a chocolate ganache with peanut butter frosting for Paulie."

Mama Dee sniffed.

Paul came out of the bathroom wearing the flimsy blue gown and a pair of not-exactly-clean socks. He climbed onto the bed. "Here we go."

They watched a half-hour TV show before Nurse Nicole came back and attached a plastic bracelet to his wrist with his name, birth date, and medical information on it.

Abby watched the nurse put a long needle into a vein in Paul's wrist.

"Does it hurt?" Abby whispered to her brother.

Mom Rachel touched Abby's arm and put a finger to her lips to tell her to be quiet.

She never told Abby to be quiet before. She usually told her to speak up.

Sorry, Abby mouthed.

"It doesn't hurt, Six-Pack," Paul said.

Nurse Nicole turned. "Who's Six-Pack?"

Abby's cheeks warmed as she tentatively raised her hand.

"That's an interesting nickname," Nurse Nicole said as she checked labels and hooked things up.

"She's an interesting person." Paul winked at Abby.

Abby sat back in the chair in the corner, glad she was there. *Paul, who plays the banjo, tells jokes, and does great in school, thinks I'm an interesting person. I write poetry. I'm crocheting an endless afghan. I have a friend in Israel and a turtle named Fudge. I guess I* am *interesting.*

"Okay, we'll get some fluids in you first, and then I'll be back to hook up your chemotherapy."

They waited an hour and a half until Nurse Nicole came back with the chemotherapy in bags she would hang on Paul's IV pole. The liquid chemo in those bags would drip, drip, drip into the tube that went into Paul's vein.

"You ready for this?" Nurse Nicole asked as she hung the first bag of chemo.

"Absolutely not," Paul answered.

"That sounds about right," Nurse Nicole said. "I don't know anyone who is. We're here to help you through all of it."

Paul nodded.

Abby imagined the medicine storming into Paul's body and fiercely battling the cancer cells. After a few minutes, Abby looked at Paul's hair to see if any of it had fallen out, and she wondered when he might throw up, because she knew those were two common side effects from chemotherapy.

But what actually happened while they sat there was . . . nothing.

Paul sat in the bed. Chemotherapy dripped into his arm. Abby and her moms talked and watched TV with Paul and checked their phones.

"Ready to go, Abs?" Mama Dee asked. "I've got to get to the shop."

"Uh, I guess." Abby wasn't ready. She wanted to stay with her brother, but she'd promised when Mama Dee was ready to leave, she'd head back to school without an argument. Abby looked at the playing cards, untouched, on Paul's table. She should have brought something different, something that would have taken Paul's mind off what was happening. Maybe she could think of something else to bring him when she visited him later.

Mama Dee kissed Mom Rachel on the cheek. "Need anything before we go?"

She shook her head.

"We'll be back by dinnertime." She leaned over, being careful of the IV pole, and kissed Paul on the forehead. "Love you so much."

"Love you too, Mama Dee."

Abby thought Paul looked so vulnerable on the white sheets in a skimpy blue hospital gown with his hairy legs protruding. She wanted to stay with him the whole time he was in the hospital, but she knew that would never fly with her moms. She'd overheard them discussing how worried they were about the schoolwork Paul would miss because of this. They'd never let her miss more school.

After making their way out of the hospital and back to the car, Mama Dee drove Abby to school and checked her in at the front office.

She'd missed only two classes.

0 0 0

Other than a boy yelling, "Watch it!" when he accidentally bumped into Abby in the crowded hall between classes, no one spoke to Abby all day. Not a teacher. Not another student. Not even the school custodian, Ms. James.

For a moment, Abby wondered if she was invisible. If maybe she was still back at the hospital and only thought she was at school.

"Abby!" It felt good to hear Conrad call her name from his spot by the fence after school.

She rushed over. "Hi, Conrad."

They fell into an easy stride walking together toward home. "How did it go at the hospital this morning?" Conrad asked while they waited for the crossing guard to give them the signal to cross.

As they stepped into the street, Abby shifted her backpack. "It was weird."

"Weird how?"

Abby stopped on the other side of the street in front of a bench. "Once Paul started getting the chemotherapy, nothing happened."

Conrad nodded and started walking again. "With my uncle, the changes didn't happen right away. It was two weeks after his first treatment that his hair fell out."

"Oh."

"And I hate to tell you this, but he actually got sicker the more treatments he had."

"Oh," Abby said again.

"Want to come over? I baked cookies last night."

Abby's heart skipped a beat. She'd been so worried about Paul, she hadn't thought as much about Conrad as usual. About how she felt when she was near him—tingly. She almost blurted a quick *Yes!* but then remembered something. "I can't."

Conrad nodded.

"No," she said. "I want to, but I promised I'd walk and feed Miss Lucy, then head right over to my mom's shop in town. We're going back to visit Paul at the hospital so Mom Rachel can go home for a while."

"Yeah." Conrad's shoulders slumped. "Makes sense."

"Or . . ." Abby held up a finger.

Conrad looked at her, hopeful.

"You could walk me into town, I mean, if you're not too busy with homework and—"

"Yes. I'll walk you into town. I can do homework later."

Abby nodded, feeling a lot better than she thought she would on her brother's first day of chemotherapy. Paul seemed okay when she'd left the hospital, and Conrad wanted to walk her into town. Even if hardly anyone talked to her at school today, it wasn't the lousy day she'd expected. Maybe Paul would be one of those rare people she'd read about on the Internet who got hardly any side effects from chemotherapy. And life could get back to normal as soon as he finished his treatments.

At Dee's Delights, Mama Dee looked frazzled. Her short hair was pressed against her sweaty forehead under her toque—the chef's hat she always wore at work. "Hi, guys," she said as Abby and Conrad walked in. "I'm not quite done yet. Mind hanging out for another half hour to an hour, and then we'll get going, Abby?"

"Sure."

Conrad tapped Abby on the shoulder. "Want to go over to Perk Up?"

Abby looked at Mama Dee, who nodded, then handed Abby a ten-dollar bill. "I'll be ready to go to the hospital when you get back."

The word "hospital" made Abby's stomach lurch. She hoped Paul was doing as well as when she'd left him.

At Perk Up, Conrad held the door open for Abby and for a woman walking in with a baby in a stroller.

The place smelled wonderful—freshly brewed coffee and newly baked muffins.

Abby ordered hot chocolate and a blueberry muffin. When she took out the ten-dollar bill from Mama Dee to pay, Conrad gently pushed her hand away. "I've got this."

Abby put the money back in her wallet, feeling like this might be a date. *Her first date. With an eighth grader!* "Thanks, Conrad."

Sitting at the table, they clinked their mugs, and Abby immediately burned the tip of her tongue with her first sip.

"So, I was thinking. . . ." Conrad had not lifted his mug to his lips.

She wrapped her fingers around the warm mug,

determined not to take another sip until it cooled off.

"Would you want to . . . ?" Conrad glanced out the window, then back to Abby. "Go out somewhere together?"

"We *are* out somewhere together." Abby regretted those words the moment they left her mouth.

Conrad looked down.

"I mean, YES!" Abby blurted.

"Really?" He looked up, hopeful.

Abby nodded.

Conrad leaned forward. "Okay, I was thinking instead of doing something ordinary, we could create . . . I don't know . . ." He leaned in even closer and said the next part quietly. "The perfect date."

Abby's heart hammered so hard, she thought it would burst through the wall of her chest. She couldn't wait to tell Cat!

"What do you think?" he asked.

Abby nodded again, even harder. Then she took another sip of hot chocolate and burned her tongue again. But at this point, she didn't care.

Conrad put his palms on the table. "And even though it's really far away, I think we should make our perfect date on Valentine's Day."

Abby's heart did three somersaults and a cartwheel. She'd never done anything with a boy on Valentine's Day before, even though Cat kissed a boy last Valentine's Day and Abby had wished something special had happened to her, too.

"Okay, we should start planning," Conrad said. "It'll be fun."

"Planning," Abby managed. "Fun."

Conrad laughed, and Abby spent the rest of the hour floating on a cloud of happiness. Even the burnt tip of her tongue couldn't dissipate her joy because by the time they'd walked back to Dee's Delights, Conrad and Abby had planned the perfect Valentine's Day date.

All they still needed to do was find someone to drive them there.

And wait.

That evening at the hospital, Paul looked the same as he did in the morning—sitting up in bed, wearing the thin blue gown with the chemo drip hooked up to an IV in a vein in his wrist. Except now his small room was filled with people—Ethan, who was inexplicably wearing a hat that looked like a chicken; Bubbe Marcia and Zeyde Jordan, who were not wearing any headgear at all; the moms and Abby; and Paul, who was playing a banjo for everyone. It wasn't his banjo from home, so it must have been the one from the teen room the nurse had mentioned.

Abby couldn't believe that being in the hospital getting chemotherapy could be fun. Leave it to Paul to figure out how to make that happen. Between Abby planning a perfect Valentine's Day date with Conrad and Paul being in such good spirits, Abby was bubbling with joy.

"Any requests?" Paul asked.

Zeyde put his hands around his mouth and called, "Can you play over the hills and far away?"

Bubbe Marcia nudged him. "Jordan!"

"What? I thought it was funny."

"It was funny, Zeyde." Paul plucked a tune, and Zeyde clapped along.

Everyone joined in the clapping, and Mama Dee tapped her toes to the music.

Nurse Nicole walked in, and up went her arms. "Didn't know we were having a party in here!"

Paul stopped playing.

Everyone got quiet.

Abby bit her bottom lip. She didn't want her brother to get in trouble; things were already hard for him. Abby wished she hadn't contributed to all the noise by clapping so loudly.

"We love parties!" Nurse Nicole shouted. "Carry on, awesome people! I'll be right back. Don't go anywhere."

"I'm sure as heck not going anywhere." Paul held up his arm with the IV taped to it.

A few people laughed.

Then Paul went back to plucking the banjo.

Nurse Nicole returned a little while later with small cups of vanilla ice cream on a tray and little wooden spoons wrapped in paper for everyone. "Can't have a party without ice cream. Am I right?"

Abby decided she was absolutely right. Also, it had to be a good sign that she'd brought Abby's favorite flavor—vanilla.

Eventually, everyone left the hospital room except Abby and her moms.

Mom Rachel stood by the bed and held Paul's hand. "I hate to leave you, sweetheart."

"Mom," Paul said. "You were here all day. You said you were going home when Mama Dee came, and here you still are."

"I know." She wiped at the corners of her eyes.

"I'm in good hands," Paul said. "Nurse Nicole will take care of me."

"She will." Mom Rachel let go of Paul's hand. "I'll be back early tomorrow."

"It's okay, Mom."

Mama Dee grabbed Mom Rachel around the shoulders and led her out, turning her head to throw Paul an air-kiss.

Abby went to her brother's side. "Can I give you a hug?"

"You'd better," Paul said.

The bed rail was in the way, but Abby reached over and hugged her brother, feeling his warm cheek against hers. "Love you, Paul."

"Love you, Six-Pack."

She gave one last wave, then ran to catch up with her moms, feeling lucky she got to leave the hospital and go home. Abby felt sad Paul had to stay in there.

When Abby and her moms got home, there was a small brown bag taped to their front door—freshly baked cookies from Conrad.

"I do believe that boy is sweet on you," Mama Dee said. "Give me one of those cookies so I can see if he's a good enough baker to spend time with our girl. Also, I'm hungry."

Mom Rachel laughed and handed Mama Dee a cookie.

They watched Mama Dee take a bite. "Mm-hmm. Crunch on the outside and soft on the inside. Not too sweet. A rich chocolately flavor. That boy passes."

Mom Rachel and Abby each grabbed a cookie as they walked in and were greeted by a very excited Miss Lucy, who didn't quite make it outside and peed on the floor.

"I'll clean it up," Mama Dee said.

"And I'll take her out." Abby hooked a leash onto Miss Lucy's harness.

"Thanks so much, you two," Mom Rachel said. "I'm thoroughly exhausted."

Abby didn't mention she was hoping to see Conrad while outside.

Conrad wasn't out there, but the mildly sweet taste of the cookie he'd baked lingered on her tongue.

The next evening, the visit to Paul's hospital room was different.

There was no party atmosphere, just Abby's brother lying in bed, looking pale, with a full tray of food pushed to the side.

Mama Dee and Abby were the only visitors in Paul's room. They'd come to relieve Mom Rachel, who'd been there all day. Abby thought Mom Rachel looked tired. And her breath smelled funky when she kissed Abby on the cheek.

"I'm going home to grab dinner and a shower."

"Take your time, honey," Mama Dee said. "We'll hold down the fort. Right, Abs?"

"Right." Abby tried to smile, but she was worried about Paul.

After Mom Rachel left and Paul, Mama Dee, and Abby talked for a while, Mama Dee turned to Abby. "I know it's late, but I'm going to buy a cup of coffee from the cafeteria. You knuckleheads want anything? Paul?" She pointed to his food tray. "Would you like me to try to find you something a bit, um, tastier?"

He shook his head. "Nah. My stomach doesn't feel too good. I'm skipping eating anything tonight."

Mama Dee raised her eyebrows. "You'll need to eat to keep up your strength for this. Plus, your stomach might feel better with at least a little food in it."

"I'm good," Paul said, but he looked like he might throw up.

Mama Dee turned to Abby. "How about you, pumpkin? Want a drink or something to snack on?"

Even though Abby was hungry, she didn't want to eat in front of Paul if he felt sick. "I'm good. Thanks."

"Okay." Mama Dee gave a salute, patted her purse, and headed out into the hall.

Abby sat on a chair at the foot of Paul's bed and chewed on her thumbnail because she felt a little nervous being in Paul's hospital room without her moms. Then she took her finger out of her mouth, thinking about all the germs that were in a hospital.

"How was school, Six-Pack? Anyone talking to you yet?"

Abby shook her head. She didn't want to discuss school. She liked walking there and walking home with Conrad, but not the lonely feelings in between. To change the subject, Abby asked, "Does it hurt?"

"What?" Paul pressed the button to raise the back of his bed higher.

"You know." Abby pointed to his wrist. "That."

Paul lifted his arm with the IV. "Nah. It hurt a little when she first put it in, but now I'm used to it." He pointed to the IV pole on wheels that the bags of chemotherapy drugs hung on. "But I don't like having to take this stupid thing to the bathroom with me. It's weird being attached to it because it has to go wherever I go. Can't wait until I'm unhooked at the end of the week and can go home. I miss my bed. And Miss Lucy. I miss the sound of frogs croaking in the canal out back."

"It's lonely at night knowing you're not in your room across the hall. Fudge misses you too."

"Aw, Six-Pack. How can you tell Fudge misses me?"

Abby bit her bottom lip. "I just know these things, Paul."

A male nurse bustled into the room and up to Paul's bedside. "Okay. Time to take your IV out."

"Huh?" Paul leaned back in his bed. "It's only Tuesday."

The nurse put on his medical gloves. "Don't worry. It won't hurt."

"I'm not worried," Paul said.

Abby thought Paul sounded worried.

"Where's Nurse Nicole?" Paul asked.

"She's helping other patients. I'm a traveling nurse. I'm helping out on this floor today."

"Wait? What?" Paul's voice rose. "I think I'm supposed to be hooked up to this all week."

The nurse smiled, like Paul was a little kid who didn't know what he was talking about.

Does Paul know what he is talking about? The nurse should know what's going on. Right? Abby wondered if she should say something and support her brother. Or maybe go look for Nurse Nicole out in the hall and ask if Paul is supposed to be unhooked from his medications this early. Abby wished Mama Dee would come back so she could handle this.

"Okay. Here we go," the nurse said, approaching Paul's IV.

"No!" Paul pulled his arm away. "Go get Nurse Nicole! She knows what's going on."

"That won't be necessary," the male nurse said. "I can take care of this. Removing an IV is a piece of cake."

"But—"

"Seriously." The nurse put a hand on Paul's shoulder. "Relax, buddy. It'll be okay."

Paul looked like he was about to punch the guy. Abby knew she should sprint into the hall and get help. Paul couldn't do it himself because he was attached to the IV and the nurse was blocking his way.

Nurse Nicole walked into the room, a big smile on her face. "My shift is ending, Paul. I came in to say—" She shook her head. "What are you doing in this room?"

The traveling nurse held up his gloved hands. "I'm removing his IV like you asked."

Nurse Nicole stepped between Paul and the nurse. "I asked you to remove the IV of the patient in room 508. That's next door."

"Oh," the traveling nurse said.

"Paul is supposed to stay hooked up all week."

"Like I was telling you!" Paul's cheeks were an angry shade of pink.

"It's okay." Nurse Nicole squeezed Paul's shoulder. "Please go next door. Into room 508."

The male nurse skirted out of Paul's room as Mama Dee came in with a paper cup of steaming coffee. "Where's he off to in such a hurry?"

Everyone stared at Mama Dee.

"What?"

"Long story," Paul said.

Nurse Nicole looked directly at Paul. "Don't you worry. He won't set foot in your room again." As she left, she mumbled, "Or in this hospital, if I can help it."

While Paul explained to Mama Dee what had happened, Abby willed her heartbeat to slow. But it wouldn't quit pounding.

"I'm so sorry," Mama Dee said. "I should have been here."

Abby's shoulders sank. She *was* here. *She* should have done something to help her brother. It was an emergency, and she'd remained quiet. Miranda and Laura might be mean girls, but they were absolutely right about her. She wouldn't speak up in an emergency . . . even if it meant saving her brother.

0 0 0

On the walk home from school Friday afternoon in the middle of October, Abby and Conrad talked about their perfect date.

"Valentine's Day seems so far away," Abby said.

"It really does," Conrad agreed. "We could always go out somewhere before then."

Abby felt an electric pulse go from her toes all the way up to the top of her scalp. "That would be nice."

"Want to come over?" Conrad asked. "To figure out where else we should go?"

Abby squeezed her hands into fists, her barely-there fingernails digging into her palms. "Can't. Paul's coming home soon. First week of chemo done. I want to be there when he gets home."

"Sure. I could come over to your house."

Abby bit her bottom lip. "I'm actually not allowed to have anyone over when my moms aren't home."

Conrad nodded. "So, how long before Paul's next treatment?"

"My mom said it would be three weeks if he was doing well."

Conrad crossed his fingers. "Hope everything goes great and he can be done with all this soon."

"Yeah, me too."

"Well, bye, Abby."

Her name sounded so good when Conrad said it. It sent a shiver racing along her spine. Abby held up a hand in a wave, hoping Conrad didn't notice the heat filling her cheeks.

As he walked across the grass between their houses, he called, "Think of something fun we could do together."

"I will."

Abby floated into the house. She grabbed a drink, then walked Miss Lucy, hoping she'd see Conrad outside, but she didn't. After spending time with Fudge, Abby worked on her endless afghan until she got bored, then grabbed her notebook and a pen.

Waiting Is Hard

Waiting for Paul to come home,
To know how he's doing,
To know if he'll get well
Is hard.
Waiting for Valentine's Day to arrive,
To have a perfect date
With a perfect boy
Is hard.
Waiting for the things that matter,
The things that change your life
For good or for bad
Is hard.

When the car pulled into the driveway, Mom Rachel hopped out and opened the back door. Mama Dee rushed around. They both supported Paul.

Abby flung the door wide open.

Miss Lucy stood at the doorway, barking and running in circles. Then she peed, and everyone had to step around it while Abby grabbed an old towel to clean it up.

"Nice homecoming, Miss Lucy," Mom Rachel said.

Abby thought she saw a faint smile on Paul's lips. He adored that dog.

"Want us to help you to your room?" Mom Rachel asked.

"Couch," Paul managed, and they supported him there.

Abby ran and got the pillow from Paul's bed and put it under his head. She knew he liked that pillow best.

"Thanks." Paul curled onto the couch, closed his eyes, and began breathing deeply.

Mama Dee put a strong arm around Abby's shoulders. "He's going to be tired for a while. The chemo really knocked him out."

It was hard for Abby to wrap her head around something as innocent-looking as a plastic bag of liquid medicine making her tall, strong brother so weak that he needed his moms to help him into the house.

"Let's let him sleep," Mom Rachel said.

As if she'd heard and understood, Miss Lucy jumped onto the couch and curled herself near Paul's feet.

"You're such a good dog." Mom Rachel patted Miss Lucy's head.

Abby worried that maybe it wasn't the chemo that made Paul look so pale, that perhaps it was the cancer and no one realized it, but she kept those worries to herself. Her moms seemed to have enough on their minds.

The two of them went into the kitchen together.

"Guess I'd better face those bills," Mom Rachel said. "Got the first one from his surgery. Whoa. I'll see if the hospital will work with us on that, maybe set up a payment plan."

"I'll make you a cup of tea," Mama Dee said.

"Might need something stronger than tea to face these bills."

Mama Dee laughed, but it had a sad echo to it.

Abby felt a stab of guilt for not helping Mom Rachel with her cooking videos. It was a small thing, but if her mom could make more videos, she'd make more money from advertisers and selling her e-cookbook, and that would help with the bills.

Miss Lucy let out a loud snore, which made Abby laugh.

Paul didn't even open his eyelids.

Abby went back to crocheting the endless afghan. It was something for her to do while she watched over Paul. He seemed to be shivering even though it wasn't cold in the house. In fact, Abby felt like she was melting with the heavy afghan on her lap as she crocheted.

That's when Abby figured out what to do with her endless afghan.

She laid it down on her chair and went into the kitchen.

Mom Rachel was at the counter with a pile of papers, her computer, a mug of steaming tea, and a giant crease between her eyebrows. She glanced up at Abby. "Need something?"

Abby shook her head and got a pair of scissors from the

drawer. "Mom, is there any way I can, you know, help out?"

Mom Rachel tilted her head, then looked at the bills. "No, honey. Your job is school. Your mom and I will take care of everything else."

I have another job, Abby thought. *Taking care of Paul.*

She went to the living room, snipped the yarn, and tied it off. Then she carefully laid the enormous multicolored afghan over her shivering brother.

Paul's eyelids flickered. He shifted under the afghan and smiled.

Abby knew her giant afghan was exactly where it was supposed to be—keeping her brother warm and comforted while he recuperated from his first round of chemotherapy.

Unexpected Moments

Exactly two weeks later, a couple days before Halloween, Abby and Paul were at the table playing Monopoly.

"Come on, Six-Pack. You know you want to buy that railroad."

"I'm trying a different strategy this time." Abby bit her thumbnail.

"What? Losing?"

"No, I'll still win." *Just not by as much as usual.*

"Okay." Paul shook his head. "I'm going to have to whup your butt and teach you a lesson about being nice."

"Oh yeah, what lesson is that?"

Paul pulled the endless afghan up higher around his shoulders. "That I will appreciate and never take advantage of you . . . except when it comes to trouncing you in Monopoly."

"Oh yeah, tough guy? Wait until—"

The doorbell rang, and Miss Lucy charged to the

window beside the door, barking her princess-y head off.

Paul raised his eyebrows.

Abby shrugged. "I'll go see."

She looked through the window and paused. Then she opened the door and stood out of the way.

Paul's voice was quiet. "Jake?"

Jake grabbed his baseball cap off his head and wrung it in his hands. "Yeah." He walked over to the table. "Mind if I sit?"

Abby had never seen Jake so . . . shy. There was absolutely no flexing of his muscles or loud, confident voice going on today.

"Nah." Paul pushed the afghan off his shoulders onto the back of the chair, and it fell to the floor, but he didn't reach down to pick it up.

Abby rushed over to get it.

Paul put up a hand. "Leave it."

Abby knew that meant she should leave too, but she gave Jake a quick stink eye for not showing up when her brother needed him. She purposely moved slowly toward her room so she could hear what they were saying.

"So, why weren't you . . . ?" Paul didn't finish the question.

"I'm sorry, man. I couldn't . . ." Jake didn't finish either.

Abby was at the door of her bedroom and couldn't hear their conversation anymore.

She sat in front of Fudge's tank and whispered, "Paul's lucky Jake came back."

Fudge opened his mouth as if he were about to offer his opinion.

"I know, little buddy," Abby said. "I wish Cat would come back too."

Abby took out her phone and sent Cat a long text.

> It's been lots of bad news and good news lately. Bad news is Paul's treatment has been hard on him. He's exhausted and cold all the time. Good news is Conrad and I are planning a perfect date on Valentine's Day. Bad news is I'm worried about Paul and how he'll get through all these treatments. Good news is his friend Jake finally showed up. Although he should have been there for Paul sooner. At least Ethan's been there for Paul through everything so far. Cat, I hope you're having a more-good-news-than-bad-news kind of day there in Israel. Miss you so much. Xoxo, Abs

Abby waited a long time, but there was no reply from Cat. Then she opened her notebook and wrote a poem she'd been mentally composing all day at school.

Alone

Sometimes you can be
Surrounded by people and their
Clanky, Clattery, Chattery
*Noise, NOISE, **NOISE!***
And still feel very quietly . . .
Alone.

0 0 0

Cat's reply came the next morning:

> Good news: I've made some new friends, and there are
> cute boys in my class.
> Bad news: Mom works a LOT of hours, and I'm by myself
> in this tiny apartment.
> Miss you, too!
> Hugs and hedgehogs,
> Cat

Abby was pretty sure Halloween would stink without Cat there, but Conrad came over to her house dressed as a basketball player—wearing a numbered jersey with a basketball under his arm.

"I know," he said. "Totally unoriginal."

"It's fine." Abby grinned and flipped on the hood of her green sweatshirt. "Guess what I am?"

"Cold?"

Abby laughed. "Nope." She was actually too warm because it still wouldn't cool off in South Florida for a couple more weeks. "Guess again."

Conrad sat on the arm of the couch. "I don't know. Kermit the Frog?"

"Ribbit." Abby flipped the hood back down. "A turtle. I'm a turtle."

He nodded slowly. "Okay. Green jacket. I get it."

She turned around to show him the turtle shell she

drew on the back of her jacket with markers.

"Now, that's cool," Conrad said.

"Hey!" Mom Rachel came out with Mama Dee following close behind.

They modeled their costumes. They were each wearing chef's hats—toques—and aprons.

"Not really a costume since you both are, you know, chefs," Abby said.

"It's the best we could do on short notice," Mama Dee said. "Hey, do you guys want to help us give out candy?"

Mom Rachel held up a big orange bowl, filled with mini candy bars.

"Can't," Abby said. "Conrad and I are going to walk around the neighborhood and get our own candy."

"Probably our last year to do that." He hunched his shoulders.

Abby thought she might be too old to go trick-or-treating, but she really wanted to go one last time. Conrad was a whole year older. He probably felt extra uncomfortable about it. "Yes," Abby said. "Definitely our last year."

"We can help you give out candy when we get back," Conrad said.

Abby hoped Conrad didn't want to rush back because he felt uncomfortable. She loved trick-or-treating, or at least she did when she went with Cat. It was fun to be in costume and pretend to be someone else for a few hours. Somehow, it helped her be more social. Of course, tonight's turtle costume would not lend itself to socializing.

"Or I can do it." Paul patted his greasy hair and wiped his nose with a crumpled tissue. "Maybe I'll scare the little kids without wearing a costume."

Mama Dee gave him a playful shove. "We'd love your help."

"But maybe you shouldn't be around all those little kids," Mom Rachel said. "Your cell counts are at their lowest point right now."

"I don't care, Mom."

"I care! The last thing you need is to catch something your body won't be able to fight off."

Paul let out an exasperated breath.

The doorbell rang.

"Okay," Mom Rachel said. "Please at least wash your hands afterward."

"I wash my hands constantly."

Mama Dee squeezed his shoulder. "We know this is tough, bud."

Mom Rachel opened the door for the first trick-or-treaters—a fairy princess and a firefighter—both girls.

They reminded Abby of Cat and her as little girls trick-or-treating together. She didn't want to think about how much she missed her friend tonight. "Let's go," she said to Conrad.

He followed Abby out into the warm evening air.

"Hey, you two!"

It was Conrad's mom, standing at the end of their driveway, holding a bowl to her waist.

Conrad held up a hand. "Hey, Mom."

"Come over," she said.

Abby followed Conrad next door. She noticed Ms. Miller's bowl was filled with Smarties and Dum Dums lollipops—the cheap candy.

"Aren't you two a little old to be going out?" she asked.

"Mom," Conrad complained.

"What? Halloween is for little kids. You a little kid?" She poked him in the shoulder.

He pulled back. "We've gotta go."

She shrugged. "Have fun, you two lovebirds."

Conrad shook his head and marched off.

Abby followed him down the street, wondering how someone as sensitive as Conrad could have come from someone who seemed so insensitive.

"Sorry," he mumbled.

"It's okay," Abby said.

They walked down their street, past all the people giving out candy, and ended up side by side on swings at the playground, where it was particularly dark. Conrad dropped his basketball in the wood chips near their feet.

The darkness allowed Abby to ask a question she'd been wondering about. "Do you ever see your dad?"

Conrad coughed. "My dad?"

Abby nodded as she gently pushed herself back and forth on the swing. "Don't answer if you don't want to."

Conrad's swing wasn't moving. He wasn't looking at Abby. "It's not that. No one ever asks me about him."

Abby swallowed hard. "Sorry. I didn't mean to—"

"Don't be. My mom and dad used to fight all the time. I remember a lot of yelling and doors slamming when I was little."

Abby couldn't imagine that. If anything, her moms were too mushy and affectionate with each other.

Conrad spoke quietly. "My dad lives in another state with another family."

"Oh." Abby turned toward him. "Do you ever get to see your dad?"

He held on to the chains of the swing and turned to look at her. "I stay over sometimes on holidays. I like it there."

"You do?"

"Yeah, it's quiet. My dad's an artist, and his wife is really nice to me."

Abby imagined Conrad's dad was sensitive like him.

Conrad jumped off his swing and grabbed the basketball. "Let's go get some candy, Turtle Girl."

So they did.

Tons of it.

When they got back, Abby's moms were outside talking with Conrad's mom at the end of their driveway. Everyone chatted for a while, then Conrad and his mom went back home. And Abby and her moms went back in and turned out their porch light because they'd run out of candy.

"Glad we finally had a chance to chat with Conrad's mom," Mom Rachel said.

"Yeah." Mama Dee sat on the couch. "Sounds like she works a lot."

Abby nodded. "Conrad says she's always picking up extra shifts."

Mama Dee took off her shoes and wiggled her toes. "It's not easy, especially as a single parent."

"True." Mom Rachel clicked on the TV. "She sounds really proud of Conrad."

That was nice for Abby to hear.

While her moms watched a TV show, Abby picked out all the Reese's Peanut Butter Cups from her Halloween candy and gave them to Paul, because they were his favorite.

The following Sunday evening in early November, Abby was working on math homework at the dining room table.

She pressed her pencil extra hard because she was frustrated. Numbers didn't make as much sense to Abby as words and their meanings. Plus, her teacher went so fast when he explained things in class, it was hard to keep up.

"Whatcha working on?" Paul asked.

Abby bit the metal around her pencil's eraser. "Word problems with variable exponents. It's confusing."

"Let me see."

Abby passed the paper to Paul, glad he was still able to help her with homework. "You nervous?"

He blinked. "About math?"

She shook her head. "About going in for your second chemo treatment tomorrow."

"Mm-hmm." He tapped the table. "I was scared to go in the first time because I didn't know what to expect. But

I'm more scared to go in this time because I do. And the effects are cumulative, so I'll probably feel even sicker this round."

Abby squinched up her nose. "I'm sorry, Paul." She couldn't imagine this getting worse and worse through four weeklong treatments.

"Hey, let's tackle this math. Okay?"

"Yeah, thanks."

When Paul bent over the paper, a clump of his hair fell onto it. It looked like a small nest of hair.

Abby gasped.

"Oh, man." Paul leaned back. "I'm so sorry."

"*I'm* sorry," Abby said in a tight voice. She felt her stomach turn, and she pushed down the urge to vomit. "Paul, that's a lot of hair right there. But I know it's not your fault. Sorry if I made you feel bad."

"You didn't. It's been falling out like that—in clumps. It's on my pillow when I wake up. It even gets in my mouth."

"Ew." Abby wished she'd stop saying the exact wrong thing. She knew Paul must already feel terrible about his hair coming out, and she didn't mean to make it worse with her reactions.

"I know. It's gross. And it's worse in the shower. That's why I haven't been washing my hair much lately. Figure I'll hang on to what I have as long as I can."

Abby had noticed how greasy her brother's hair had been. It made her sad to think about why he hadn't been washing it.

"Guess I'd better get used to the fact that it's going to fall out no matter what I do. Maybe I should shave it off and get it over with."

"That sounds drastic. Could you wear a hat to keep it on or something?"

"Not sure that's going to work, Six-Pack."

Another dumb idea, Abby. Maybe it's time to stop talking.

"Let's just do this math. Okay?"

Abby nodded.

Paul explained the problems to Abby, but as hard as she tried to focus, she couldn't concentrate on what he was saying because she kept waiting for more of Paul's hair to fall out in gross clumps. And thinking about that instead of paying attention to him when he was helping her made Abby feel like the worst sister in the world.

Round Two

As Abby and Mama Dee walked from the parking lot to the hospital's entrance, Abby noticed pink layers sweeping across the light blue sky as the sun set. A soft breeze rustled palm fronds on tall trees near the hospital's entrance.

It's beautiful out here, Abby thought. *And Paul is stuck inside.* She wondered if he was at least watching the sunset from his room. Wondered if his room faced the west so he could watch it at all. She hoped so. But even if he were, he wouldn't be able to feel the coolness in the breeze that told her the season's heat had finally broken and cooler weather had arrived. He couldn't smell the hint of ocean with its salty scent that tickled Abby's nose.

Abby wished she could capture it all and bring it inside to her brother or bring him outside to experience it, but he was hooked up to his chemotherapy, so he wasn't going anywhere other than his bed, the bathroom, or on a slow shuffle-walk down the hall to the teen lounge.

It's like he's a prisoner, Abby thought.

As soon as the hospital's automatic doors whooshed open, air-conditioning hit Abby's skin, which made it prickle with goose bumps. And instead of smelling faintly of the ocean, the hospital smelled faintly of bleach.

Even the bright, cheerful decorations on the way to Paul's room didn't lighten Abby's heart. The happy "Hello!" from a couple of the nurses didn't lift her mood one bit.

All the fun decorations in the world and the kind staff couldn't change the fact that this was a sad place. Abby felt that sadness deep in her heart. She knew Paul must feel it too.

As Abby and Mama Dee walked into Paul's hospital room, Ethan was walking out.

"Hey there, Abs!" Ethan gave Abby a hug.

This made her feel a little better. *At least Paul has been surrounded by people who love him.*

"Our guy's doing okay in there," Ethan said.

But Abby thought Ethan's smile seemed strained. She could feel the sadness in him, too.

"Glad you're here," Mama Dee said, pounding Ethan on the back. "You're a good friend."

Abby thought Mama Dee might have wanted to say that Jake should be here too, because he should. But Abby hadn't seen him since that one time he came over to the house when she and Paul were playing Monopoly.

Ethan nodded. "I've got to go to my job now, but I'll visit again soon."

"Thank you," Mama Dee said. She took a deep breath

and squeezed Abby's hand, and they walked into the room together.

In the hospital room, Mom Rachel was in the chair by the foot of Paul's bed. Paul was sitting up in bed with a pink plastic pan on his lap. His hair was gone now—he'd finally asked Mama Dee to shave it off when it was looking sparse and awful—and he was wearing the stupid baseball cap with the squirrel holding its acorns. Abby stared; she was trying to get used to her brother without hair, but he seemed like a stranger.

"Take a photo. It'll last longer," Paul said.

Abby shrank back. "Sorry."

Mama Dee made a face. "Be nice to your sister, mister. It's a lot to get used to."

"It's a lot for *me* to get used to." Paul gagged and lifted the plastic pan toward his mouth, but then leaned back. "This sucks so bad."

"It does," Mom Rachel said. "It really does, sweetheart."

"I want to be home. I want to feel better." He lifted his arm with the IV attached and dropped it back down onto the bed like he didn't have the energy to hold it up a moment longer. "I want this stupid thing out of my arm."

"I know, honey." Mom Rachel squeezed her hands into fists. "I know you do."

Mom Rachel flashed Mama Dee a look that Abby thought meant this was harder than any of them had expected.

Paul made a strange gurgling noise, then a stream of vomit erupted from his mouth and splashed into the pink pan on his lap.

"Oh." Abby pressed herself against the wall and looked out the window. The sun had already set. It was getting dark. Paul had missed the whole beautiful thing. And it didn't smell like the ocean in his room; it smelled like puke.

Abby turned back toward her brother.

Paul swiped an arm across his mouth. "Get her out of here!" he managed before a volcano of vomit erupted all over his blanket.

"Take her," Mama Dee said, gently pushing Abby toward Mom Rachel. "You go home and get a break. I'll stay here."

Mom Rachel nodded and steered Abby out of the room.

They stopped just outside the door.

Abby could still hear Paul retching. She hunched her shoulders, as if she could hitch them high enough to cover her ears and block out the horrible sound.

Mom Rachel grabbed a nurse nearby. "My son will need some help in there."

The nurse headed into Paul's room.

Mama Dee slipped out and hugged Mom Rachel. They rocked back and forth.

Mom Rachel pulled back and bit her bottom lip. "He's been vomiting like this for a while. They said he'll get some medicine in his IV that should get it under control, but . . ."

Mama Dee held Mom Rachel again.

Reaching a hand out, Mama Dee grabbed Abby's fingers and gave a reassuring squeeze.

Mom Rachel cried on Mama Dee's shoulder. "The doctor said Paul's getting every side effect in the book this time. She doesn't know how we'll get him through all his treatments."

Mama Dee held Mom Rachel tighter. "We'll find a way."

Mama Dee's voice sounded strong and sure. Abby wanted to believe her. But then Paul vomited again, which elevated the worried feeling in Abby's stomach. The nurse in his room spoke calmly, but Abby couldn't make out her words.

"I'd better get back in there." Mama Dee gave Mom Rachel and Abby one more squeeze and then slipped back into the room.

Mom Rachel put an arm around Abby's shoulders and sniffed. "Let's get you out of here, sweet pea. We'll visit again when your brother's feeling better."

Part of Abby couldn't wait to get out of that hospital, but another part of her wanted to stay in Paul's hospital room the entire time he was there so he'd never be alone. But even Paul didn't want her there now. He had yelled for her to get out, which hurt her heart.

Abby felt guilty the moment the automatic doors opened and she escaped into the cool, clean air with her mom. All Paul wanted to do was leave the hospital, and he couldn't. "It's not fair," Abby said.

"No, it's not," Mom Rachel replied. "It's definitely not."

As soon as Abby got home, she went into her room and texted Cat to tell her what had happened.

Even though she knew Cat was probably sleeping, Abby kept checking her phone for a response. Eventually, she slid it under her pillow and fell asleep.

The phone's ringing woke Abby in the morning.

"How are you?"

Cat's voice filled Abby's tired brain with love.

"Thanks for calling."

"Of course I called. How are you doing?"

Abby started crying. Everyone was so concerned with how Paul was doing; it was nice to have someone care about her. "I miss you so much." What Abby held back saying was *I need you.*

"You have no idea how much I wish I were there," Cat said. "Especially with what's going on with Paul. I hate being so far away, Abs."

After Cat had to go, Abby still had time before Conrad would come over to walk to school together, so she pulled out a pen and her journal—because it made her feel closer to Cat—and she told the truth on the page.

Alone and Scared

Paul is there,
Alone and scared
Wishing he could be home.
I am home,
Alone and scared
Wishing I could be there.
I will find a way
To be **strong**
For Paul,
For me.

One Thing to Be Thankful For

Exactly two weeks later on Thanksgiving night, Abby found herself in her bedroom talking to Fudge, which was only slightly better than talking to herself.

"Thanksgiving stunk," she told him. "Paul's close to his nadir, which means he's super susceptible to infections. So none of our family came over, not even Bubbe Marcia and Zeyde Jordan, and I miss them. I wanted to show Bubbe a turtle hat I crocheted from a cool pattern I found online. It came out looking like a lopsided dinosaur, but I know she'd still like it."

Fudge swam around his tank, unconcerned about Abby's problems.

But Abby wasn't done talking. "Both moms were exhausted, so we ate peanut butter and pumpkin butter sandwiches and canned cranberry sauce. We've never eaten canned cranberry sauce in our lives. It held the shape of the can when it plopped out. It tasted too sweet and was slimy and weird. Nothing like Mom Rachel's homemade cranberry sauce with whole cranberries in it and a delicious orange flavor."

As Abby's turtle kept swimming, it was obvious to her that Fudge couldn't care less.

"Thanks for nothing." Abby dropped onto her bed, trying to think of one thing she was thankful for. Just one.

Suddenly, banjo music floated from Paul's room. Light, fun banjo music. She hadn't realized how much she'd missed the sound of it—how her heart had missed those upbeat plucky, plinking sounds.

Abby put her hands behind her head and let out a relaxed breath. "I'm grateful Paul is well enough to play his banjo and that he's home and not in the hospital."

Then she looked over at Fudge. "But a real Thanksgiving meal with all our family here would have been nice too."

He turned and swam away from her.

The Sunday after Thanksgiving, Abby had something else to be thankful for—a date with Conrad. The idea came to him, he told her, after he visited the public library and read a poster about a teen board game day.

Ms. Miller drove Conrad and Abby to the public library and dropped them off at 2:45 p.m. "You sure your moms are able to pick you two up?" she asked Abby. "I'm off today and I could get you."

"Thanks, Ms. Miller," Abby said. "My mom said she'd pick us up right before the library closes."

"Awesome. Maybe I'll get some holiday shopping done. Have fun, you two."

Abby was glad she didn't say *Have fun, you two lovebirds*, because that would have been embarrassing.

Conrad probably appreciated it too, because he said, "Thanks, Mom," in a really nice way, and Ms. Miller smiled.

In the library's community room, folding tables and chairs were set out, and board games were piled on one table near the wall.

"Thanks for coming to this," Conrad whispered to Abby as they walked in.

"It sounds like it'll be—"

"Welcome!" A cheery librarian with short blond hair and rosy cheeks walked over. "You're here for the teen board game program. Right?"

Abby and Conrad nodded.

"Great. I'm Miss Amanda. You can go pick any game you like and start playing. Pizza should be here soon." Miss Amanda glanced up at the clock. "And I'm sure some other kids will be here soon too."

Abby secretly hoped no one else would show up. It would be fun to have the whole room to themselves . . . and Miss Amanda.

When they were at the pile of games, Abby ran her fingers along the boxes—Stratego, Life, Clue, Battleship, Scrabble, and many more. She wanted to take her time and choose carefully. She was looking for something both she and Conrad would enjoy that wasn't too easy or too complicated. Something—

"This one okay?" Conrad had plucked out a game.

When Abby saw what he'd chosen, she was surprised by the emotions that flooded through her. *How come I didn't notice that game right away?*

"Abby?" Conrad sounded alarmed. "Everything okay?"

She nodded. "Paul and I usually play that one."

"Oh, we can choose something else. There's a ton of games here."

"I love Monopoly."

"You sure?"

Abby appreciated how thoughtful he was of her feelings. "Only if I get to be the dog."

"That's cool because I like the race car."

"Perfect."

And it was. Conrad put the box on one of the tables, and they set it up together in an easy rhythm.

When the pizza arrived, Abby took one slice and put it on a sheet of paper towel the librarian had laid out. Conrad ate two slices, and Miss Amanda had one, and there were still three and a half boxes of pizza left over.

They were well into their game when Miss Amanda asked, "You two want more pizza?"

"No thanks," they both said.

"Guess I'll bring this to the staff room."

Abby and Conrad barely noticed they were alone in the large room because they were so absorbed in their game.

"I'm going to bankrupt you, Braverman!"

"You wish, Miller! Now pay up. You landed on my property."

"Was hoping you wouldn't notice that."

At 4:30 p.m., Miss Amanda stood beside their table. "The program is supposed to end now, but you can keep playing until the library closes."

"Thanks," Conrad and Abby said without looking up from the board.

When the announcement was made over the loudspeaker that the library would be closing in ten minutes, Abby and Conrad counted their money and the value of their houses, hotels, and properties.

"I won," Conrad said. "Told you I'd beat you, Braverman. I'm the Monopoly Master!"

Abby was glad he didn't go easy on her. She reached out her hand, and Conrad shook it. His hand was a little bigger than hers and warm. "You beat me . . . this time, Miller. But I'm going to win next time."

"Whatever you need to believe, Braverman."

They cleaned up the game.

"Did you two have fun?" Miss Amanda asked.

"Yes. Thanks!" Abby said.

"This was great," Conrad said.

Then they walked out of the library and got into the back seat of Mom Rachel's car.

"Behold the reigning Monopoly champion." Conrad pumped his hands in triumph.

Abby shook her head. "He won this time, Mom. But I'm totally going to teach him a lesson next time." And she gave Conrad a poke in the ribs.

"Ouch!"

Then the two dissolved into heaps of laughter in the back seat.

Abby noticed in the rearview mirror that Mom Rachel was smiling. She hadn't seen her mom smile in a while.

"I'm taking you two out for ice cream sundaes."

"Awesome. Thanks, Mom. Should we bring some back for Paul?"

"That would be really nice." Mom Rachel tapped the steering wheel to the beat of the music on the radio. "I'll get a scoop of chocolate marshmallow for Mama Dee, too."

They drove toward the ice cream parlor, happy, each of them knowing to appreciate such a splendid day amid the difficult ones.

Round Three

Paul's third chemotherapy treatment was scheduled for a week later, on a Monday—the last day of Hanukkah.

Since Paul was beginning to feel better—he seemed to feel well right before he had to go back into the hospital for another treatment—the moms planned a Hanukkah celebration for the Sunday before, and the entire family was invited.

"I'll finally get to see my cousins," Abby told Fudge. "And I can show Bubbe the hats I've been crocheting. The most recent one almost looks like a turtle. Like you!"

Fudge dipped his head under the water as if to say, *Big deal.* He apparently did not share Abby's enthusiasm.

Paul was not wearing his cap when everyone arrived.

His head was bald with tiny nubs of hair beginning to sprout.

Abby had gotten used to seeing her brother without hair, but her cousin Jared kept staring at him. She almost told him to "take a picture; it would last longer," but she didn't want to make Jared feel bad.

Abby sat close to her bubbe on the couch, showing her the most recent hat.

"If you did your stitches a little differently here and here, I think it would look more turtlelike," Bubbe Marcia said.

Abby considered the changes and decided her bubbe was right. She'd make one more attempt and buy the soft green yarn she saw in the store last week. "Thanks, Bubbe."

"Anything for my *shayna punim.*"

Abby melted into her bubbe's side, feeling safe and loved.

Paul was in the great room with Cara and Elyssa, who were trying to teach Miss Lucy to lie down and roll over. Abby thought it was a waste of time trying to teach that dog anything other than sitting for a snack and going to her bed. But when she heard a cheer from the great room, Abby knew they'd succeeded.

Zeyde Jordan leaned across Bubbe Marcia and tapped Abby on the knee. "Okay, smarty-pants, I have a science joke for you."

"Let's hear it," Abby said.

"Why can't you trust atoms?"

Abby bit her bottom lip. "I give up. Why?"

"Because they make up everything!" Zeyde roared.

Uncle Steve cupped his hands around his mouth. "Booooooo!"

"Let's hear another one," Aunt Jeanne prompted.

"Don't encourage him," Uncle Steve warned.

Abby examined her turtle hat, deciding how she'd use Bubbe's suggestions to make it better on the next try. She couldn't wait to buy the yarn in town. She knew exactly what she was going to do with the hat, if it came out right.

Zeyde said, "Okay. Why did the banana go to the hospital?"

When no one responded, he said, "Because he was peeling really bad."

Everyone was silent.

"Get it? Peeling really bad?" Zeyde offered.

Bubbe Marcia elbowed him. "They get it, Jordan. *Sha!*"

Abby was glad Paul was in the other room and missed the hospital joke. She was more glad when Mom Rachel called, "Dinner's ready, everyone!"

The potato latkes were delicious, especially with Mom Rachel's homemade applesauce, but Abby noticed Paul ate only half a latke.

Bubbe sat next to him. She put a hand on his shoulder. "*Nu, bubbelah?*"

"Sores in my mouth, Bubbe," he said quietly. "It hurts to eat."

She patted his hand. "All this will be behind you soon."

"Can't wait," Paul said, and slumped in his chair.

Zeyde Jordan was mostly quiet at dinner, which was unusual. He kept looking over at Paul and sighing.

Mama Dee noticed Abby staring at Zeyde. She tapped Abby's shoulder, leaned close, and whispered, "Paul's cancer is hitting your grandfather hard."

Abby nodded and whispered back, "I think it's hitting everyone hard."

Mama Dee grabbed Abby's hand under the table and squeezed.

Christmas morning, Cat texted Abby.

> I'm totally missing going out with you and your family to Mr. Zhang's for Chinese dinner, Abs. How am I supposed to live without those spring rolls and duck sauce? Mom made brussels sprouts for dinner. BRUSSELS SPROUTS.

Abby laid down the turtle hat she was almost finished crocheting and responded.

> The moms said we wouldn't be going out for dinner tonight anyway. Paul's susceptible to infections. We're staying home. All the holidays have stunk this year.

> That does stInk, Abs. I'm sorry. He'll be done with treatments soon, and things can get back to normal. Right?

Abby hoped she was right, but it felt impossible. Paul seemed like a different person, and Abby wasn't sure the old Paul was still there to come back after treatments. But that was all too much to say in a text, which was why Abby missed being able to talk to Cat in person. Even video chats were always interrupted by Cat's mom.

Yeah, I'm sure you're right. Gotta go.

Love you, Abs.

xoxoxo

Abby didn't really have to go, but texting with Cat made her miss her even more, and Abby was already sad about Paul being so sick and being unable to go out for Chinese food like they always did.

Nothing was the same anymore.

When another text came in, Abby was sure it was from Cat. She didn't feel like texting with her anymore but checked her phone anyway. The text was from Conrad.

Hey, Sleepyhead. You ready to exchange gifts? I've got to leave soon to go to my uncle's house.

Abby leaped up.

Give me ten minutes.

The clock starts now, Braverman.

Abby liked that Conrad called her "Braverman" sometimes. He was the only person who did, so it felt special.

She grabbed her favorite sweater—purple with black stripes—because it was chilly outside. Then she threw on jeans and her Converse sneakers. After brushing her teeth and hair, Abby reached under her bed and pulled out the gift she'd made for Conrad. Then she ran to the door.

When she opened the door, Conrad was standing there, leaning on a column and tapping his wrist, where a watch might be. "You're late, Braverman."

"I have, like, four minutes left." Abby grabbed his arm and pulled him into the house.

"Hi, Conrad!" Mom Rachel yelled from the kitchen.

"Hey!" he yelled back.

Abby and Conrad sat on the couch.

Mom Rachel came out, wiping her hands on a towel, with a dish under her arm. "Merry Christmas, sweetheart."

"Thanks, Ms. Braverman."

Mom Rachel handed him the dish that had silver foil wrapping on top and a bright red bow. "Mama Dee baked these brownie bars for you and your mom. We're so glad you're living next door."

"Thanks!"

"And please thank your mom for the nice dinner she dropped off the other day. It really made things easier for us."

"Will do."

Miss Lucy hopped up onto the couch, sniffed the dish, then snuggled next to Conrad.

Smart dog, Abby thought.

After Mom Rachel went back into the kitchen, Conrad leaned over and whispered to Abby, "I didn't think to get anything for your moms."

His breath smelled like peanut butter. "They don't want anything," she whispered back.

"Okay. But I did get this for you." He handed Abby a small wrapped box.

"Thanks, Conrad. It's perfect."

"You didn't even open it yet."

Abby felt her cheeks flame. "Oh, yeah." She gently pulled off the paper. It was a box of magnetic poetry tiles, and on the front of the box, the tiles were arranged to say, YOU TOTALLY ROCK. "You totally rock!" Abby blurted.

She could see Conrad's cheeks go pink, and she realized they were both embarrassed. "I mean, uh . . ."

"Well, I'd better get going. Mom's waiting to go to my uncle's. He promised to play basketball with me."

"Basketball!" Abby shouted. "I made you something. I mean, I made your gift."

Conrad raised his eyebrows. "Is it something I can eat?"

"Only if you want to choke to death." Abby shook her head. "I didn't mean—"

"Abby!"

"Yeah?" She bit a thumbnail.

"Calm down."

She nodded and handed him a small bag. "It's just a little thing. I didn't know. I thought maybe—"

"I'm sure it's great." Conrad pulled away the tissue paper from the little bag and pulled out an orange crocheted circle with a key ring attached. "It's a . . ."

"Basketball key ring." Abby pointed out the black stitching that made it look like a basketball. "I saw how to make it online."

"It is a basketball key ring!"

"Yup. I told you it's small."

"Abby?"

"Yes?"

"I love it." He reached into his pocket and put his house key on the key ring. "But I've really got to go."

"Conrad?"

He stood and turned to look at Abby. "Yeah?"

"Merry Christmas."

"Merry . . . Hanukkah?" he offered.

Abby lit up like a menorah on the eighth night.

They hugged, and he left.

Abby sat on the couch, holding the box of magnetic poetry tiles to her chest. "It is perfect," she whispered.

Mom Rachel came out with two limeade spritzers and handed one to Abby. "You know, I really like that boy," she said.

"Yeah. Me too."

"And his mom has turned out to be a good neighbor. I mean, nobody could replace Miriam, but I'm glad she's a nice person."

Abby nodded, thinking about her bubbe's saying about a door closing and a window opening.

Late that afternoon Abby, Paul, and Mom Rachel were sitting together in the living room.

Mom Rachel handed Abby a menu from Mr. Zhang's. "Let me know what you want. Mama Dee will run out and pick it up."

Abby chose two spring rolls and vegetable fried rice. She

knew it wouldn't be as much fun as going out to the restaurant, but at least they'd be having Chinese food together on Christmas like always.

When Abby passed the menu to Paul, he handed it back to Mom Rachel.

"You have to order something, Paul," she said.

He shook his head.

"I'm getting you a spring roll. Surely you can eat one spring roll."

"Mom."

That was all he said, but it was enough to make her stop talking and put the menu on the table.

Even though Paul was huddled under the endless afghan and Miss Lucy was squished up beside him, he shivered.

Abby understood that his low blood cell counts meant that he didn't get enough oxygen and it made him cold. "I'm sorry the endless afghan isn't enough to keep you warm."

He nudged his shoulder into hers. "It's the best, Six-Pack."

Hearing her nickname felt good.

"I'll turn up the heat." Abby ran from the room and nudged the thermostat a bit warmer. Then she went into her room and grabbed the turtle hat she'd just finished crocheting. "Hi, Fudge," she said to her turtle, who was warming himself under the lamp.

She didn't wait to see if he responded in any way. Abby was already back in the living room. "Here." She handed the hat to Paul. "It's really soft, and it'll help keep the heat in.

I read online that seven to ten percent of body heat escapes through your head."

Paul put the hat on.

Mom Rachel's laughter bubbled out.

Abby laughed too.

Paul pulled out his phone, turned on the camera, and looked at himself. "Not bad," he said. "I look like . . . a turtle."

"You really do." Abby beamed and sat beside her brother. "But in a good way."

"Who looks like a turtle?" Mama Dee walked into the room. When she saw Paul, she staggered back with her hands up. "Who is that handsome turtle over there?"

Paul shook his head, and Mama Dee grabbed the menu. "Everyone make their choices?"

No one said anything.

"Oooookay," Mama Dee said.

Mom Rachel leaned over and patted her hand. "We're all set, babe. Just add one spring roll to what everyone wrote down."

Mama Dee called in the order while the rest of them sat quietly.

Suddenly, Paul asked, "Mom, how's the channel doing?"

Mom Rachel looked up, surprised. "*Lettuce Eat?*"

He nodded and tugged the turtle hat on a little tighter.

"Well," Mom Rachel said, "honestly, it's not as popular since your handsome mug hasn't been on there."

Paul looked down at his lap.

"Oh, Paul. I didn't mean . . ."

"Sorry," Paul said quietly.

Abby moved closer to her brother.

Mama Dee put down her phone. "What are you sorry about, Paul? What did I miss?"

Paul looked up. His eyes had dark circles under them. His skin looked especially pale with no eyebrows on his face. "I'm sorry for keeping you both . . . from work. I'm sorry I can't help . . . Mom with her videos."

Abby's heart broke at how her brother struggled for breath to talk. She squeezed her hands into fists, which she wanted to use to smash the entire universe for all of its unfairness. She wished she were stronger, able to help her brother more somehow. But she just sat there—useless—plain old Abby.

"Paul," Mom Rachel said. "We don't care about those things."

Paul swallowed and grimaced. "I care. I know I'm making everything . . . harder for . . . everyone. And I'm especially sorry for . . . costing so much money and making you have all those . . . bills. I'm—"

"Don't you dare, Paul Braverman." Mom Rachel sniffed and wiped her eyes. "Don't you even . . ."

Mama Dee sat next to her and held her close.

"I'm sorry I haven't been able to play Monopoly with you, Six-Pack."

Abby bit her bottom lip so she wouldn't cry.

He huddled small under the giant afghan with the silly turtle hat on his head. "I'm sorry I got so . . . sick and can't do . . . anything for myself . . . or anyone . . . else . . . and . . . you all have to take . . . care of . . . me." Paul sobbed and shook.

Miss Lucy barked, then climbed into his lap and lay down.

Mama Dee rushed over and sat where Miss Lucy had been. She squeezed Paul around the shoulders and leaned her head next to his. "We love you, buddy, and you have nothing to be sorry for."

"Absolutely nothing." Mom Rachel came over and sat by Paul's legs, resting her head on his knees.

Abby squished in closer. She loved her family so much, even if it felt like they were breaking apart. No matter how much they loved Paul and no matter what they did, they couldn't keep him from having to go through this. The only thing they could do was stay beside him during all of it no matter how hard it was to bear.

Later at Mom Rachel's request, Paul ate a total of one spring roll for dinner. No duck sauce.

Exactly nine minutes later, he ran to the bathroom and vomited it back up.

Mom Rachel put her head in her hands. "I shouldn't have . . ."

Abby stood behind her mom and massaged her shoulders. "It's not your fault." She felt more like the parent than the kid. "It's the medicine's fault."

Mom Rachel reached up and patted one of Abby's hands.

"He'll be okay, Rach," Mama Dee said.

Mom Rachel nodded but didn't lift her head.

Abby helped her moms with the quick cleanup from dinner, then went to her room.

Even with her bedroom door closed, she could hear Paul vomiting and both moms in there with him, murmuring soft words. Abby imagined them rubbing his back and telling him he'd be okay soon.

"Cancer is hard," she told Fudge.

Fudge solemnly sat on his rock in complete agreement, Abby was sure.

Needing a place for the feelings swirling inside her, Abby pulled out the journal from Cat, ran her fingers over the cover, opened to a fresh page, and wrote.

Before and After

One day my brother said, "I have cancer."
With those words—that one word—
Oxygen left the room
Sound
Molecules
And then came back, forever rearranged.
Nothing has been the same since.
There is only before . . . and after.

A New Year

A week later on New Year's Eve, Abby sat with her moms in the living room.

Paul was in his room with Ethan. Every once in a while, Abby heard banjo music coming from the room. And laughter.

"Here's to a better year ahead." Mama Dee raised her glass of champagne.

"Hear, hear." Mom Rachel raised her glass.

Abby raised her glass too, because the moms said she could toast the new year with a tiny bit of champagne.

They all clinked glasses.

"Paul should be out here with us," Abby said.

"Ah, let's let him have time with his friend," Mom Rachel said. "He gets enough of us."

Abby wasn't sure what her mom meant by that.

"Yeah," Mama Dee said. "That boy should be out with his friends doing fun stuff, and instead he's stuck in the house or the hospital all the time, feeling rotten."

Mom Rachel raised her glass. "Here's to Ethan . . . for showing up and taking Paul's mind off things."

"To Ethan," Mama Dee said. "And we hope that Jake gets a splinter the size of Kentucky stuck in his tuchus on the same day he gets a zit the size of Alaska on his nose."

"Dee!" Mom Rachel laughed, then covered her mouth.

"What? I used 'tuchus' right. Didn't I?"

"You did," Mom Rachel said. "You're bad."

"And proud of it!"

Everyone laughed.

Abby sipped her champagne, and the bubbles made her want to sneeze. She did not like the taste but drank the small amount her mom poured for her anyway. She didn't get why adults liked to drink alcohol. It tasted gross.

Later in her room, Abby texted Cat, even though she knew it was too late for her to answer.

I still miss you.

A few minutes later, a text came through.

What are you doing?

It was from Conrad.

Nothing.

He replied immediately.

Can you come out front for one minute?

Abby held the phone out and looked at it.

Why?

She waited, but there was no reply. Abby checked the time. It was 11:58 p.m.

When she went out to the living room, she saw that her moms had fallen asleep with Miss Lucy between them. It was really cute.

Abby opened the front door.

"What?" Mom Rachel had woken and opened one eye. "Where are you going?"

"Right out front. I'll be back in one second." Abby closed the door behind her before her mom could say anything else.

"Oh!" Abby startled.

Conrad stood in front of her on the porch. "Sorry. Didn't mean to scare you." But the way he was smiling, Abby thought maybe he was pleased with himself for startling her.

Abby moved from foot to foot. It was chilly out, and she hadn't thought to throw on a jacket. "You surprised me, that's all."

"Surprises can be good. Right?"

Abby tilted her head. "Um . . . right."

Conrad looked at his watch. "I just wanted to wish you a happy new year."

They both stood there.

He checked his watch again. "It's midnight."

Conrad stepped forward and kissed Abby.

His lips were soft and warm, and his breath smelled minty.

"Happy New Year, Abigail Braverman. I can't wait for our perfect date on Valentine's Day." Then Conrad ran back home.

Abby's lips tingled. She touched her fingertip to them, wondering if the feeling was from the champagne earlier or from Conrad's kiss. She was pretty sure it was from the kiss. She didn't even get a chance to wish Conrad a happy new year because he ran away so fast.

Someone down the street was banging pots and pans and shouting, "Happy New Year!"

Fireworks went off in the distance.

When Abby turned to go back in, the door was wide open. Her two moms were standing there, grinning.

Abby was grinning too.

She hugged them both and went back to her room, lay in her bed, and watched Fudge swim around his tank.

Abby had a lot to think about.

She'd had her first New Year's kiss.

It was perfect.

Maybe it would be a good year, after all.

Round Four: Emergency!

A few days later, Paul and the moms planned to leave early for Paul's fourth and final chemo treatment at the hospital.

Abby had set her alarm so she could see them off.

When Abby had asked if she could go to the hospital with them, Mama Dee said, "You have to go to school. One kid in this house missing tons of school is more than enough. Thank you very much."

"Absolutely," Mom Rachel agreed. "You can visit your brother after school."

When Abby woke the morning of Paul's final treatment, it was dark outside, and the frogs in the canal were still croaking their nighttime chorus.

Abby shuffled to the kitchen, where Mama Dee slurped coffee from her favorite mug—a blue ceramic one she got when she and Mom Rachel took a vacation a couple years ago to a bed-and-breakfast in New Hope, Pennsylvania.

Mom Rachel was packing a small cooler bag with snacks. Miss Lucy lay curled up in her bed in the corner of the great room, snoring softly. Paul sat on a stool at the counter, his head on his hands. He wore the crocheted turtle hat over his bald head, which Abby thought made him look silly. And sweet.

Abby put her palm on her brother's bent back. She could feel his spine protruding because he'd lost so much weight. "Last one," Abby said in the most enthusiastic voice she could manage this early in the morning.

"Mm-hmm," Paul answered with all the energy of a stale potato chip.

When they were ready to leave, Abby leashed up Miss Lucy and walked her family to the car.

Abby held the back car door open for Paul.

He slid onto the seat, buckled his seat belt, and let out a sad sigh.

Abby leaned in, gave her brother an awkward hug, handed him an envelope with a poem she'd written earlier, and whispered in his ear, "You've got this, Paul. I love you."

Miss Lucy barked.

"The princess loves you too," Abby said.

He looked up and gave his sister a half smile.

Abby knew it was the most he could offer, and it would have to be enough. She wished Paul were stronger, but Abby would have to muster her courage and be strong enough for both of them for now.

As Abby watched her family drive down the street, gentle

strands of pink laced through the dark sky, like wispy signs of hope.

Back inside, Abby made herself a fruit salad with slivered almonds sprinkled on top and a mug of chai with coconut milk for breakfast. She fed Miss Lucy some smelly wet food in her fancy dish. Miss Lucy thanked her by thumping her tail over and over again. "You're welcome, girl." Abby pet Miss Lucy's silky ears. "You're doing a good job of looking out for Paul."

Miss Lucy responded by peeing on the floor.

"Yeah." Abby cleaned up the mess, and while waiting for Conrad to pick her up for school, Abby wrote a poem in her journal.

Endings and Beginnings

The end.
Because one story ends
Doesn't mean another doesn't begin.
This ending is really . . .
Paul's beginning.
His new life without cancer. (I hope.)
His happily-ever-after. (I hope.)
His new story, filled with promise. (I hope.)
Once upon a time . . .

Abby was sitting at the back of the room in language arts class when it happened.

Ms. Petroccia was reading the last chapters of *Bridge to Terabithia*. She'd been reading a few chapters every day near the end of each class.

Abby loved being read to. It was much more satisfying to lose herself in the world of a story than to be forced to do group projects with her classmates, who were not her friends.

While Ms. Petroccia read, a couple boys had their heads resting on their arms on their desks. Abby wondered if they were listening intently or sleeping. Miranda and Laura looked like they were hiding their cell phones behind their desks. Probably texting each other instead of paying attention to the beautiful story.

Their loss, Abby thought. *Bridge to Terabithia* was becoming a favorite book, like *Charlotte's Web*, which Paul had read to her when she was younger.

Abby listened to Ms. Petroccia read about Jess and Leslie and their friendship, which made her miss Cat. But it also made Abby think about Conrad and how glad she was that they'd become friends . . . and a bit more than friends.

The sadness of the story had caught Abby by surprise. She wasn't ready for what happened to Leslie. Abby didn't mean to, but as Ms. Petroccia read, Abby's shoulders hitched. She cried out loud with one great, gulping sob. It was so embarrassing, but Abby couldn't stop sobbing. The story had also made her think about Paul and everything they'd been going through. It reminded her that people die—even young people.

Abby wished she were a turtle and had a shell to hide inside, but she was just a girl, her deepest emotions exposed right there in class.

Kids turned to look at her, to see where the choking, gasping, sobbing sounds were coming from.

A few boys lifted their heads from their desks.

One boy chuckled.

It's not funny! Abby wanted to scream.

"So sensitive!" Miranda said, waving her hand dismissively at Abby.

"Yeah," Laura said. "It's just a story, Abby. Get it together."

Abby faced the front and took a shaky breath. She wasn't crying anymore. She was focusing on Ms. Petroccia. And she could hardly believe what she was witnessing. Ms. Petroccia was up there crying too. Her teacher wiped her cheeks with a tissue and closed the book. "I read this story to my classes every year, and still it makes me cry. It's that powerful."

Abby looked around the class. Turns out, she wasn't the only one sniffling, crying, and wiping at her eyes. Plenty of her classmates were crying and tearing up too.

Not Miranda and Laura, but many others.

Kyle Baxter leaned over and said to Miranda and Laura, "I think Abby is just the right amount of sensitive. That was a super sad story." And he blew his nose into a tissue.

Abby sat a little taller. She let Kyle's words roll around in her mind. *I think Abby is just the right amount of sensitive.* Abby had never thought of being sensitive as an asset. She'd never thought you could be the right amount of sensitive.

But maybe you could. Maybe she was. Perhaps her sensitivity made her a more empathetic and understanding person when someone was going through a hard thing. Maybe it made her a better friend, daughter . . . sister.

"Hey, Six-Pack," Paul said from his seat at the dining room table as soon as Abby walked into the house after school.

She stumbled backward. "What . . . what . . . are you doing home?"

Paul tipped his baseball cap—the one with the squirrel and acorns. "I escaped from the hospital."

"You what?!" Abby dropped her backpack and joined him at the table, accidentally bumping Miss Lucy—who was under the table—with her foot. "That dog sticks to you like glue."

Paul smiled. "She's a good dog."

"He's kidding about escaping from the hospital," Mom Rachel called from the kitchen.

"I'm kidding," Paul said. "The real story is much more boring. My cell counts were too low to get the chemo. So I'm home instead."

Abby got excited. "Does this mean you don't have to get any more chemo?"

Paul's hopeful look deflated. "I wish. It means I have to wait until my cell counts come back up to get my fourth and final round. And I'm going to save that envelope you gave me until then."

"Oh." Abby felt the disappointment in her gut.

Mom Rachel called out from the kitchen, "And he has to get a shot every day for a week to help his cell counts climb back up."

"Don't remind me." Paul rubbed his upper arm.

"Hey!" Mom Rachel called. "Either of you knuckleheads want to help me make a *Lettuce Eat* video?"

Paul shook his head. "I'd scare away viewers looking like this," he called to Mom Rachel.

"Oh, Paul!"

Then he leaned toward Abby and whispered, "You should help her, Six-Pack."

Abby shook her head. "I want to, but I'm not brave like you."

Paul leveled her with a stare. "I'm not brave, Six-Pack. I'm scared to death most of the time."

Abby was shocked. "But look at what you're going through. That takes courage."

"Nope." Paul adjusted his cap. "Didn't really have a choice, so that's not courage. Being brave is when you're scared to do something but you choose to do it anyway because you know it's the right thing to do."

Abby thought about that. *It's when you're scared to do something but you choose to do it anyway because you know it's the right thing to do.*

When Abby heard, "Welcome to *Lettuce Eat*. Today we're going to make a delicious vegan sweet potato and black bean chili," Abby got up. She walked into the kitchen. "Sorry for interrupting, Mom."

Mom Rachel turned off the recording. "That's okay, sweetheart. I can restart it. What do you need?"

"I want to help." She glanced into the other room and saw Paul give her a double thumbs-up. "I mean . . . if that's okay."

"Okay?" Mom Rachel squeezed Abby for all she was worth. "That would be wonderful."

Abby ran her fingers through her hair and pulled her shoulders back. "I'm ready."

Mom Rachel explained to Abby what they'd be cooking and what parts Abby could help with on the video. Then she hit the record button. "Welcome to *Lettuce Eat*, where we'll be making a delicious vegan sweet potato and black bean chili. We have a special guest with us today—my daughter, Abby."

Abby looked right into the camera and waved. "Hi! I'm Abby, and I'm so glad to be here with you today. Ready, Mom?"

"Ready, Abs!"

Abby helped her mom make the meal and even managed to sneak in a joke or two, like Paul would do. Abby couldn't wait to tell Cat. And Conrad. And when the video came out, she'd try not to pick out all the things she felt like she did wrong. She'd let it be exactly what it was—Abby being imperfectly, perfectly brave. And if some of the viewers didn't like it, that was their problem. Not hers.

Paul's cell counts had climbed high enough that he was able to get his chemotherapy the Monday of the following week. His final treatment. The hardest one.

On the third night Paul was in the hospital, Abby went with Mama Dee to visit him.

Paul was sleeping with the light on and the TV playing. Abby noticed the poem she'd given him in the envelope lying open on his table.

World's Best Brother

Paul, when I was younger,
You read me Charlotte's Web
And cried at the end,
Which let me know it was okay
For me to cry too.
You made me French toast
And took me to the movies
When Cat left for Israel,
Which let me know
You'd always be there for me.
You went through difficult
Surgery and treatment for cancer,
Which showed me what strength looks like
And how I can be brave by facing hard things.
You also make me laugh
And smile
And feel better about myself.
Not everyone gets a terrific brother like you.
Not everyone can say their brother is a friend.
You're the world's best brother, Paul.
I love you!
—Abigail Rebecca Braverman (aka Six-Pack)

Abby grinned because her brother was wearing a pair of green short-sleeved pajamas with little squirrels and acorns all over them. Ethan had given Paul the pajamas as a joke because it reminded him of the Pin the Nut on the Squirrel game they'd played the night before this all started. Of course Paul wore them. Anything for a laugh. The turtle hat Abby had crocheted almost matched the pajamas perfectly. Thick blue socks with little white treads on the bottom covered Paul's feet. Since the pajamas were shorts, Abby could see that Paul's once-hairy legs were completely smooth. Paul's bare legs somehow made him look young and vulnerable. Abby had a fierce urge to protect her brother and keep him safe.

"They put him on a new medicine," Mom Rachel told Mama Dee.

"Another one?" Mama Dee planted her hands on her sturdy hips. "He's already on so many, Rach."

"I know. This one's called Ativan. It's supposed to make it easier on him with all the vomiting."

Mama Dee filled her right cheek with air, and then let it escape. "Well, he sure could use help with that."

"It doesn't make him not vomit," Mom Rachel explained. "The doctor said the Zofran is for that. This Ativan will sort of make it so he doesn't remember it."

Mama Dee's brow furrowed.

"I'm skeptical too. But the doctor thought it would be a good idea."

Mama Dee squinted, like she didn't believe the doctor.

"But maybe this medicine isn't such a good idea because he hasn't been himself since they put him on it," Mom Rachel said. "Burst out crying twice today for no reason."

"That's not like our Paulie at all. He's usually the one trying to make everyone laugh."

Mom Rachel looked over at Paul, still sleeping in the hospital bed. "It was so strange. Nothing was wrong. He just couldn't stop crying. He was so out of it. I'm going to talk to the doctor about it tomorrow."

Mama Dee let out a breath. "This has been so hard to watch."

Mom Rachel grabbed Mama Dee's hand and nodded.

Abby felt her stomach tighten. She knew if Paul woke up crying for no reason, it would scare her.

"I hate to leave him, but I'll run home, take a quick shower, grab something to eat, and be right back. I'm going to sleep here tonight since he's been so out of it."

Mama Dee squeezed Mom Rachel's shoulder. "Of course, Abby and I will be here until you get back. Take your time."

Mom Rachel gave Abby a kiss on the cheek. "I feel like we keep passing each other like this. Is everything okay in your world, Abs?"

Abby nodded.

"Hey, the video you helped me with is getting a lot of views and thumbs-ups. A bunch of people are commenting that they want to see you in more videos."

"Really?"

"Really."

"That's cool." Abby reminded herself to check out the video later when she got home.

Mom Rachel touched Abby's cheek with the back of her hand. "Really appreciate your help, Abs." Then she slipped on her jacket and grabbed her purse. "Okay, then. If you two have everything covered here, I'm out."

"We're good." Mama Dee grabbed Abby's hand and squeezed.

Abby watched her mom leave.

Mama Dee and Abby sat there awhile, but Paul slept soundly while the IV dripped, dripped, dripped medicine into his arm.

"Baby girl," Mama Dee said, "I'm going to run to the cafeteria and grab a cup of coffee before I fall asleep like your brother over there. You want anything?"

Abby's stomach seized as she remembered how the last time Mama Dee went for coffee, that traveling nurse nearly unhooked Paul from his chemotherapy. She looked at her brother. He hadn't even shifted positions since they'd arrived. "I'm okay," Abby said. *But please hurry back.*

A minute later Abby heard the elevator ding and knew her mom was on it, heading down to the cafeteria.

Paul shifted.

He opened his eyes.

Abby lifted a hand. "Hi."

Paul squinted at her, then started crying. Big, choking sobs.

"Paul?" Abby leaned forward, panicked.

He sniffed hard. "I . . . I . . . have to pee."

"Okay. You don't have to cry about it. I'll help you." Abby looked at the IV pole he was attached to. "What do you need me to do?" She didn't want to help her brother use the bathroom. That would be too awkward. "Should I get a nurse? Do you want to wait until Mama Dee comes back? She's just getting coffee."

Paul sniffed hard and stopped crying. "No. I have to go to the bathroom right now." He looked at the plastic bags hanging on the pole. "All this liquid makes me keep having to pee."

Paul swung his legs around and put his socked feet on the floor. As soon as he stood, his legs collapsed and he went down, arms flailing.

"Paul!" Abby stood and saw her brother lying on the floor beside his bed with blood spurting and spraying all over him. "Oh my . . ."

Paul moaned with his eyes half-closed. "It hurts! It hurts!"

Abby saw Paul's arm was free. The plastic piece was still taped to his arm with blood coming out of it, but the rest of the tubing wasn't attached anymore. The chemotherapy wasn't going into his arm, and blood was spurting and splattering everywhere—the wall, the floor, the bed, Paul.

Even onto Abby!

It had splattered all over the poem she'd written for him.

Paul tried to stand but fell again hard on his rump. "Argh!"

Abby's breathing came in gasps.

"Ohhh," Paul moaned. "It hurts."

Do something! Abby told herself. *If there were an emergency, would you be quiet and let people die?* Abby's legs trembled, and her feet felt like they'd grown roots into the floor, keeping her from moving.

Being brave is when you're scared to do something but you choose to do it anyway because you know it's the right thing to do. Abby suddenly understood she could be quiet and sensitive *plus* brave and bold at the same time. That's what Abby 2.0 really meant.

She didn't want to leave her brother struggling on the floor, blood spurting everywhere, but she knew she had to.

Abby darted into the hallway, hoping she'd see Mama Dee coming toward her holding the familiar cup of coffee, but the hallway was empty. "Help!" Abby screamed, but it came out as a croak. She found a stronger, braver voice and bellowed, "Help! Help! I need help right now!"

A nurse came running from a patient's room and held on to Abby's shoulders. "What's wrong?"

"My brother. Blood. Everywhere." Abby led the nurse into Paul's room, hoping her brother hadn't bled to death while she was out getting help.

"My God." The nurse ran back into the hall. "Help in 514! Stat!"

Soon another nurse ran in.

Abby got out of their way, pressing herself against the wall, watching as they got Paul up and back into bed. The first nurse cleaned his wrist and was able to get the IV back in, then they worked together to clean up the blood.

So much blood. It ruined Paul's cute new pajamas.

Paul was crying again. "I just wanted to go to the bathroom. I need to pee."

"You're on Ativan," the nurse said. "You have to call someone to help you next time. Do you understand?"

Paul nodded, tears streaming down his cheeks.

Mama Dee walked in holding her coffee cup. She was whistling softly until she saw the mess that was Paul and the nurses working on him. "What the . . . ? What happened?"

One nurse took Mama Dee into the hall and explained while the other continued to clean up and help Paul finally get to the bathroom.

While all this was going on, Abby said something to herself she knew to be true. *I saved my brother. Miranda and Laura were wrong. I would speak up in an emergency. I may be quiet and sensitive, but I'm also strong and brave when I need to be.*

Mama Dee returned to the room, shaken.

It frightened Abby to see her big, strong mom pale and trembling. She was the one who usually held everyone else together.

"He'll be okay now," Abby told her.

Mama Dee bowed her head, and then she looked Abby right in the eyes. "He will, but I'm sorry. I'll never leave you alone with him in here again." Mama Dee rubbed at a bloodstain on Abby's shirt. "We'll try to get that out when we get home."

"It's okay." Abby was talking about the blood splatters on her clothes.

"No, it's not," Mama Dee said. "You shouldn't have had to deal with this by yourself. It'll never happen again, Abby. I promise."

Abby nodded, but she knew deep in her heart that even if her mom did leave her alone and something happened, Abby would do whatever she had to. She would be brave, like her last name—Braverman.

As soon as Abby got home, she threw out the clothes she'd been wearing, because even if Mama Dee could get the blood out, Abby knew the clothes would remind her of this horrible day and she didn't want that. Then Abby took a long, warm shower; got into comfy pj's; and then texted Cat.

Worst night ever! But Paul is okay, and so am I.

It was no surprise that Cat didn't reply; Abby knew she must be asleep. So Abby did something that made her at least feel closer to Cat. She pulled out the journal she'd given her, opened to a clean page, and wrote a poem.

Being Brave

Being brave
Is mixed with being scared.
You can't have one
Without the other.
Being scared

Isn't a choice.
But being brave
Is a choice.
Today, I was scared.
And I'm so glad . . .
I was also brave.
I'm Abby 2.0 and
Plain Abby, too—brave
When I need to be.
And scared sometimes too.
All parts of me.

"Good night, Fudge," Abby said to her turtle after she put away her journal and turned out the light.

She could hear him swimming through the water in his tank.

Abby couldn't fall asleep for a long while. She kept playing the incident over in her mind. It was hard knowing Paul wasn't in his room down the hall, but Abby was glad Fudge was there beside her, keeping her company and watching over her.

"Turtles do important work in this world," she whispered into the darkness.

An Ending. A Beginning?

Two days later on Friday evening, during Paul's last minutes of his last treatment, his hospital room was full again, like it was at the beginning of his first treatment.

Paul wasn't crying or confused because he'd been taken off the Ativan right after the accident.

Zeyde and Bubbe were there with their arms around each other's waists, along with Mom Rachel, who was wearing a PAUL KICKED CANCER'S BUTT! T-shirt over bright purple yoga pants; Mama Dee, in her usual black slacks and button-down white shirt; Aunt Jeanne; Uncle Steve; Ethan; Abby; and Nurse Nicole.

Everyone wore a pointy party hat, even Abby.

Paul put his party hat on over his crocheted turtle hat, because he said it would hurt if he put it directly on his bare scalp. "Think I could get a job as a male model?"

"Absolutely," Mama Dee said.

Nurse Nicole, who was also wearing a party hat over

her tight blond curls, stood next to Paul's IV pole. "You ready for this?"

"So ready," Paul said. "And to be a sport, I'll try not to commemorate the occasion by vomiting on your shoes."

"My shoes appreciate your thoughtfulness, Paul."

Abby loved that Paul was joking around. It showed that the spark inside him was still there. Her brother might look different from the Paul she knew before he started treatment, but he was the same inside, where it mattered.

Abby quickly texted Cat so it would feel like she was part of the big moment too. If she weren't in Israel, Abby knew Cat would be standing beside her in the hospital room, and they'd probably be holding hands as Paul was disconnected from his last chemo drip.

> **Paul's finishing his last day of the last chemo treatment right now!**

It was 11:25 p.m. in Israel, so Abby didn't expect a reply, but one arrived.

> **Hooray for Paul! I knew he could do it. Now he'll keep getting better and better. Love you, Abs. G'night.**

It still sounded funny to Abby when Cat said "G'night" and it was only early evening for her. She hoped Cat was right, that Paul would keep getting better and better. She'd read about people who thought they were fine after treatments and then the cancer came back. Abby looked at her brother, seeming small in his hospital bed, and wondered if she'd ever not worry about him again.

"Everybody else ready?" Nurse Nicole asked. "Count it down with me, Paul's people. Ten . . . nine . . ."

Everyone in the room joined in.

Paul grinned. He looked like a little boy about to get a birthday present.

". . . three . . . two . . . one!"

Nurse Nicole disconnected Paul's IV and removed the needle from his wrist.

He shook his arm. "I'm finally free!"

A cheer went up from the room.

Zeyde Jordan let go of Bubbe Marcia's waist, waved his hands like he was conducting an orchestra, and started everyone singing "For He's a Jolly Good Fellow."

Abby wondered if all the noise was bothering other patients. There were some really sick kids on the fifth floor. Maybe they didn't want to hear a celebration.

Another nurse wheeled in a cake that read, PAUL KICKED CANCER'S BUTT!

It matched Mom Rachel's T-shirt.

Mom Rachel nudged Mama Dee. "It's perfect, babe."

"We've got to celebrate our boy. And what better way than with cake?"

They hugged.

"I want the 'butt' piece," Zeyde Jordan said, and everyone laughed.

◍ ◍ ◍

On the drive home, Abby expected Paul to be exuberant. He was finally able to get back to living his life. It was like he'd been released from a prison sentence. But when Abby glanced over at her brother, he was biting his bottom lip and looking out the window.

Abby thought Paul looked a little lost.

Isn't he happy to be going home?

Hard Truths
and a Painful Plaque

Abby squished next to Mama Dee on the couch while crocheting a new hat for Paul to wear until his hair grew back. It was a plain blue hat with very soft wool, so it wouldn't irritate Paul's bare scalp. His turtle hat was looking kind of ratty and had a couple spots of dried blood on it from the accident.

Mama Dee was thumbing through a pastry cookbook with full-color photos of delicious desserts that were making Abby's mouth water.

Miss Lucy plopped herself on top of Abby's feet, which kept them warm and only gave her a little feeling of pins and needles.

Abby laid her crocheting in her lap. "How come Paul's sleeping so much?"

Mama Dee looked up from her cookbook. "His body's recovering from the chemo, Abs. Those drugs were an assault on his body. Sleeping will help his body recover, help him build back his strength."

"But he's really sleeping a lot. Like, three naps a day."

Mama Dee patted her leg. "Keep crocheting that hat for him. He'll love it. And he'll be okay."

Abby nodded, but she worried he wouldn't be okay because he seemed to be getting worse instead of better. She wondered when his hair would grow back and when he'd be his old self, like he was in the hospital right before he got disconnected from the chemotherapy. Conrad had said his uncle was working and playing basketball after he was done with chemo. Paul was . . . sleeping.

On the third day after he got home from the hospital—Monday—Paul came out of his room and sat on a stool at the counter next to Abby, who was doing homework.

"It's so good to see you up, Paul," Mom Rachel said, an apron covering her overalls. "I made those veggie burgers you like. I'll set a plate up for you."

"Can't eat," Paul said.

Mom Rachel leaned on the counter. "But you have to eat, honey. I know you're worried about throwing up, but you have to try. You've lost so much weight."

Paul looked down at himself and made a sour face. "Please," he said. "I know you love cooking and you're trying to help, but stop trying to feed me. Right now, everything tastes like metal, and it's ruining my favorite foods." He pulled a crumpled tissue from his pocket and wiped his nose. "Besides, I still have sores in my mouth and throat. It really hurts to eat."

It really hurts to eat.

Those words stabbed Abby's heart. She put her pen down.

There had to be a way to help Paul. *How can he eat without it hurting his mouth and throat?* Abby remembered when she'd had a tooth pulled and Mama Dee took her out later that day for a vanilla milkshake. It made her mouth feel better and tasted delicious. "Would a shake be better until the sores heal?" Abby was sure Mom Rachel could make him a delicious shake filled with healthy foods.

Paul looked at his sister. "Thanks, Six-Pack. Good idea, but right now I only want . . . to go back to bed."

He shuffled to his room and closed the door behind him.

Mom Rachel looked at Paul's closed bedroom door, and her shoulders drooped. Then she looked at Abby. "He'll be fine."

Abby knew her mom didn't believe what she'd said. And Abby didn't believe it either.

What if the chemo damaged Paul in some way and he never gets better? What if the cancer isn't gone?

The following Friday—the third week in January—when Abby got home from school, the house was quiet, except for Miss Lucy's dog tags jangling as she ran to greet Abby and sniff her sneakers.

Abby gave Miss Lucy a small treat, then grabbed a banana and a glass of tangerine juice for herself.

Mom Rachel came out of her bedroom, wiping at her eyes.

"Mom?" Abby asked, afraid something terrible had happened to Paul.

"It's nothing," Mom Rachel said. "How was school?"

Abby raised her eyebrows. It was obviously something. And Abby didn't want to talk about school right now. "Mom, what is it?"

Mom Rachel nodded toward the living room, and Abby followed her there, holding her glass of juice but not drinking it.

They sat on the couch, and Miss Lucy jumped up and plopped down between them.

Mom Rachel fiddled with a button on her overalls. "Your brother refused to see his tutor today."

"You mean the guy from the school district who comes to the house?"

"Mm-hmm."

"Then how's Paul going to get through eleventh grade? He can't go back to school yet. Can he?"

"No, he can't. That's why he needs the tutor." Mom Rachel threw her hands up. "And he's not eating enough. I can see each of his ribs. It's like he's disappearing, and there's nothing I can do about it."

Abby didn't like seeing her mom this way. "What should we do?"

"I don't know. That's the problem. I'm sorry to dump this on you, Abs. Mama Dee's still at the shop, and I'm so upset." Her mom started crying again. "I thought it would be hard to get Paul through treatments, but then we did it."

Abby patted her mom's hand. "We did."

"No one said it would be this hard after the treatments were over."

Moving closer to her mom without squishing Miss Lucy, Abby gently put an arm around her mom's shoulders.

She never did get a chance to tell her mom about what happened in school. If she had, Abby would have mentioned that she read an original poem out loud in front of all the kids in her language arts class. Afterward, on the way back to her seat, Kyle Baxter gave her a high five while the class applauded. After Abby sat down, Miranda leaned over and said, "That was a good poem, Abby."

Abby realized she and Paul were both changing. She was becoming Abby 2.0, which was really just the best version of who she already was. And Paul, it seemed, was becoming less like himself every day.

Later, when Conrad texted to ask if Abby felt like going for a walk, she threw on a jacket and dashed outside, glad to escape the sadness in the house for a while. She didn't feel bad about leaving because Paul was in his room sleeping, as usual. It's not like she would have been keeping him company if she'd stayed home.

Conrad and Abby walked all the way to town without saying anything.

Abby loved how they could be together without talking and it felt comfortable.

They didn't stop at any of the stores in town but kept walking.

It was getting dark, but Abby didn't want to turn back. She felt calmer being with Conrad. Happier.

They ended up in a neighborhood Abby wasn't familiar with. The homes were bigger than in the neighborhood where they lived. There were a lot of open spaces with grass and palm trees. One grassy area had a bench under a big tree and pretty streetlights around the space.

Conrad sat on the bench and patted the seat beside him.

Abby sat, feeling a spark of energy being so close to him. "How far do you think we walked?" she asked.

"Couple miles." Conrad kicked at the thick grass.

Abby sensed something was bothering him, but she didn't want to pry. She'd let him talk when he was ready.

They were quiet together for a while, and then Conrad said, "My dad asked me to spend spring break with him and his family."

Abby turned his words over in her mind and was ashamed her first thought was a selfish one about how much she'd miss him. "How do you feel about that?"

Conrad sighed. "It's kind of hard."

Abby didn't say anything, to allow him space to keep talking.

"I like being there. His wife is nice to me, but I watch my dad do all these things for my half brother and half sister." Conrad looked down at his lap, where his fingers were clasped tightly. "Things he never did for me."

"Oh," Abby said.

"Yeah. It's like he's figured out how to be a great dad for them, but what about me? Why didn't I get the great dad, instead of the one who fought with my mom all the time and couldn't wait to leave us?"

Abby pressed her shoulder against Conrad's. "That sounds so hard." She felt lucky to live with two parents, who loved her and Paul and who loved each other.

Conrad turned to Abby. "Sometimes when I'm there, I don't want to come home. My dad's more like me, or I'm more like him."

Abby nodded because Conrad didn't seem much like his mom.

"My dad likes cooking and poetry like I do. My mom hasn't read a book in, like . . . I don't even know when. She comes home from work and watches her shows or talks to her girlfriends on the phone. And once, when I read her a poem I really liked, she laughed at me. Laughed! Told me I was so much like my dad, it was scary."

Abby could picture Conrad's mom acting this way. Also, poetry? He liked poetry? How had she not discovered this sooner?

Conrad looked up to the dark sky, as though there might be some answers written up there among the twinkling stars. "When I'm at my dad's, we go to art museums and this great old library with marble columns out front. I love it, but it makes me sad, too. That makes no sense. Right?"

Abby felt honored that Conrad shared these personal feelings with her. That's what real friends did when they trusted each other. "Of course it makes you unhappy. It must be hard to see the life you wish you had but don't."

"Wow."

"What?" Abby was afraid she'd said something wrong,

something to upset him after he put his trust in her.

"You nailed it, Abs. That's exactly what it is. It's the life I wish I had, but . . . I'm here with my mom, and I don't feel like she gets me. At all."

"Maybe you and your mom are really different people, but I'm sure she loves you."

"We are different, and I know she loves me. I love her, too. But sometimes I wonder what life would be like if I lived with my dad instead."

Abby looked down.

"What?"

"Then I'd never have met you." Abby thought about how empty her life would be without Cat *and* without Conrad, especially while going through Paul's cancer treatments.

Conrad nudged his shoulder into hers. "That part would stink." He sat taller and looked at Abby. "I'm glad to know you, Abigail Braverman. You're definitely one of the best things about moving here."

The compliment overwhelmed Abby, and she giggled. Trying to deflect the praise, she said, "I'm sure you've made plenty of friends at school, but thanks."

"No, I haven't."

"Huh?" Abby thought she'd heard him wrong.

"You're pretty much my only friend."

"I . . . I . . . had no idea." *Real friends trust each other with the truth.* "You're my only friend too, Conrad."

He nodded. "Well then, it's a good thing we have each other."

"It really is."

They were both quiet for a long while, shivering occasionally from the cool breeze, but neither one suggested they go home.

Abby couldn't believe how much she'd just learned about Conrad. She knew she'd spend a lot more time thinking about some of the things he'd said. It must have been hard for him to talk about his parents and not having friends at school. "Thanks for sharing all that stuff with me." She bumped her shoulder back into his.

"Thanks for listening."

Abby beamed.

"You want to walk back now?" Conrad asked.

Abby wished she could stay on that bench with him forever, but it was dark and getting chillier. "Okay."

When they stood, something made Abby look at the bench they'd been sitting on, and she noticed a plaque affixed to the back of it. It glistened in the light of a nearby streetlamp. Abby bent and squinted so she could read the words on the plaque.

THIS BENCH IS DEDICATED TO NATHAN LAURENCE

GREENE, AUGUST 11, 2006–SEPTEMBER 19, 2020—

A BRIGHT LIGHT EXTINGUISHED TOO SOON.

Abby's hand flew to her mouth. "He was only fourteen."

"Who?"

She pointed to the plaque, and Conrad leaned over and read it too. "Wow. That's horrible."

They began their walk toward home. "How do you think he died?" Abby asked, her voice a whisper.

Conrad shrugged. "Car accident? Cancer?"

Abby inhaled sharply.

"Oh, I'm sorry, Abby. I didn't mean . . ."

Tears pooled at the corners of her eyes. "It's . . . it's . . ."

Conrad grabbed her arm and gave it a reassuring squeeze. "Paul's going to be okay. He is."

That's when the waterfall let loose. Abby shook her head. "He's not. He's not acting right. He's not getting better."

"That's from the chemo."

"Huh?" Abby stopped walking and found a tissue in her pocket to wipe her eyes and nose. It reminded her that Paul was always wiping his nose. He said his nose ran all the time because he didn't have nose hair anymore.

"It happened to my uncle," Conrad said.

For a moment, Abby thought he was talking about his uncle's nose also running all the time, like Paul's.

Conrad continued. "I remember how worried my mom was after his treatments were over. He seemed really sick for a couple weeks afterward, and then he slowly got better."

"Are you sure?"

"A hundred percent."

"But what if Paul doesn't . . . get better?"

"He will."

"But . . ."

They walked the rest of the way home with only the wind whispering in their ears and the sounds of crickets and occasional croaks from frogs to keep them company.

Breakfast

The next morning, Saturday, Abby got up early. She had a plan.

Quietly, she went to the kitchen and put on her mom's apron. It was too long on her, but she didn't care. Abby made sure to soak the slices of French toast in the egg mixture a long time so they'd be really soft. When everything was cooked and smelling delicious, Abby placed a plate of French toast with sliced strawberries on a tray, along with a glass of coconut milk. She poured syrup into a small container, so Paul could put on the amount he wanted. Then she carried the tray to Paul's room and knocked on the door with her foot.

No answer.

Balancing the tray with one hand, she opened the door.

Her brother was huddled under the endless afghan, only his head with the new crocheted blue hat showing.

"Paul?" Abby whispered. "I made you French toast."

He mumbled and rolled onto his back.

Abby thought her brother looked so vulnerable, lying there, blinking at her without eyelashes.

"Hello?" The tray was getting heavy.

"Yeah, yeah. Come in, Abs." Paul sat up in bed and leaned back against his pillow. He yawned.

Abby put the tray on his desk. "I made you French toast."

"I see that."

"And I soaked it a long time so it wouldn't hurt the sores in your mouth."

"Thanks. It smells really good."

Abby smiled. "I used the good cinnamon from Penzeys. Do you think you can eat it?"

Paul scratched his head through the hat. "You sound like mom."

"Which one?"

Their inside joke didn't feel as funny today.

Paul wasn't reaching for the food. He looked so washed out. Even though Conrad said her brother would be okay, Abby wasn't sure if she could believe him. *What if everyone is wrong? What if he never gets better?* Abby thought of the plaque on that bench. *What if . . . ?*

Abby lunged toward the bed and grabbed Paul around the neck. She pressed her head to his and whispered fiercely, "Oh, please don't die, Paul."

"Abby!"

She pulled back.

"Sit."

Gently, Abby sat on the edge of Paul's bed and sniffed.

"First of all, I'm not planning to die."

"But—"

"That's why I went through all this. The surgery. The chemo. My cancer doctor says she's almost positive all the cancer is gone. I'll get a PET scan soon to be sure, but that's a really positive sign."

Abby released a shaky breath.

"What I seem to be having trouble with"—Paul rubbed a hand over his chin—"is figuring out how to live."

"You're . . ." Abby couldn't wrap her mind around what her brother had said. Why would he have to figure out how to live? Wasn't that something you just did?

"Now that this is all over, the get-well cards have stopped coming, the calls of support. The visits. Even Ethan hasn't stopped by lately. It's like, okay, Paul is done with treatment, so we can get on with our lives now. But I'm not sure how to get on with mine. I feel kind of . . . stuck." He ducked his head. "Scared."

"Oh, Paul." Abby recognized that her brother was trusting her with his truth, like Conrad did when they sat on that bench with the heartbreaking plaque. She wanted to respect that by not saying anything stupid.

"I'm also really sad, but I'll figure it out. And I'm not going to die, so stop thinking that."

Abby looked down. "Okay. Good."

"Six-Pack?"

"Yeah?"

"Give me that tray. I'm starving!"

A Purr-fect Date

Three weeks later, on Valentine's Day, Abby's phone woke her with a chime.

She was sure the text was from Conrad, reminding her to bring something or other for their perfect date. But it wasn't. It was from Cat.

> I thought I'd miss you less as time went on, but I still miss you, Abs. Hope you have the world's best Valentine's Day. Wish we were there together, making cookies and laughing our heads off. You'd better tell me every detail of your date with Mr. Magnificent . . . or else. Kisses and kangaroos, Cat

A sadness tugged at Abby's heart. It was so strange to think that it took her best friend leaving for her to have met Conrad. *When a door closes, a window opens.* Abby wished she could have the door and the window open at the same time. But she was glad she could share everything happening with Conrad with Cat by text and during their video chats. It made her feel closer to Cat. It must have been horrible a century ago, when all people could do was send letters to each other and wait weeks in between for a reply. Abby squeezed her cell phone, grateful for the technology that allowed her to reply to Cat right away.

> **Miss you too, Cat. You'll always be my best friend, no matter where you live. Hope you and your mom have a happy Valentine's Day. If you kiss any Israeli boys, you'd better tell me about it right away! (And I'll tell you every detail about my date today, but I'd better get ready for it now.) Hugs and hummus, Abby**

Then another text came in.

Should I bring cookies? My mom bought eight packages from Publix. They were on sale.

Abby laughed and replied.

> **Cookies are good.**

It wasn't the same as baking cookies with Cat like she had done last year, but it was nice in a different way.

As Abby headed to the bathroom, Paul was coming from his room.

"Hey," she said. "You've got some hair growing back on your head."

Paul rubbed the top of his head. "Yeah, some fuzz going on. But I wish my eyelashes would hurry and grow back. You have no idea how many little particles get into your eyes without eyelashes."

"Is that why you blink a lot sometimes?"

Paul laughed. "Hadn't realized I was doing that. But yeah, I guess."

"Never thought about how important eyelashes are to keep stuff out of your eyes."

"Why would you?"

Guilt stabbed at Abby. She didn't have to think about all the things Paul did. She didn't have to deal with the challenges he did, and she never would. It's not like Abby could ever get testicular cancer. It's not like she could truly understand what Paul had gone through and was still going through. "Paul?"

"Yeah?"

"You can use the bathroom first."

"Thanks. I'll be quick."

"One more thing."

He turned toward her with his hand on the bathroom doorknob. "Yeah?"

"Happy Valentine's Day."

Paul's shoulders sagged. "You know what I woke up thinking about this morning?"

Abby shook her head.

"Last year on Valentine's Day, Jake and I had promised each other we'd have girlfriends by this Valentine's Day. We swore it on a stack of our old X-Men comic books." Paul laughed, but it wasn't a funny laugh. "Now, not only don't I have a girlfriend on Valentine's Day, but I don't have Jake, either. It sucks."

"It does." Abby leaned against the wall, feeling bad because she was super excited about today. A year ago, she could have never imagined she'd be going on a date on Valentine's Day. "Does Jake even text you or anything?"

Paul shook his head. "Guess it's hard to know who's got your back until you go through something like this."

"Paul?"

"Yeah?"

"I've got your back."

"I know you do, Six-Pack."

But Abby knew it wasn't enough. There were some things Abby wasn't able to provide for her brother, no matter how much she wished she could. Losing a friend was hard, especially if you lost that friend when you needed them most.

Abby was checking to make sure she had everything in her backpack when the doorbell rang. Her heart jackhammered.

Miss Lucy charged to the door, barking.

"I've got it," Abby told her. "You're a good guard dog, but way too small to be intimidating. Plus, when you roll over to offer guests your belly, you lose all credibility."

Miss Lucy kept barking.

When Abby flung open the door, Conrad stood there, head tilted to the side, hair over one eye. "Happy Valentine's Day, Abigail Braverman." He handed her a card.

Abby pushed Miss Lucy out of the way with her foot while she accepted Conrad's card. "Thanks. Let me get yours." She was so glad she'd thought to make a card for Conrad. She would have felt awful if he gave her one and she had nothing for him.

"Hey, Conrad!" Mama Dee called from the kitchen.

"Hello!"

As Abby ran out of her room, holding the card, Mama Dee said to her, "I need to make one quick phone call about an order for the shop, and then we can get going."

"Awesome. Thanks so much for driving us."

Mama Dee cupped Abby's cheek with her palm, then got a little misty while looking at her.

"Mom!"

"I can't help it." Mama Dee gave Abby's shoulder a squeeze. "You're growing up, and I can hardly stand it."

"Shhh." Abby pointed toward the living room, where Conrad was waiting for her.

Sorry, Mama Dee mouthed, then hustled into her bedroom to make the call.

Back in the living room, Abby gave Conrad a handmade card with a turtle on the front. She had used her favorite colored pencils to draw it, using three different shades of green and dark brown. It was her best drawing of a turtle to date.

"Nice artwork." Conrad nodded. "Didn't know you could draw."

Abby waved away the compliment. "Only turtles. I'm sort of obsessed."

"Good to know. That does explain your Halloween costume." Conrad read the card aloud. "'I just wanted to shell you . . .'" He raised his eyebrows at Abby.

For a moment, she thought he was just showing off because he had eyebrows to raise. "Open it," Abby said. "It gets worse."

He did and read the inside. "'I'm not too cold-blooded to give you warm wishes for a Happy Valentine's Day.'"

"Get it?" Abby asked. "Turtles are cold-blooded and—" She realized she sounded like Zeyde Jordan when he explained one of his silly jokes.

"Oh, I get it." Conrad clutched his heart. "You're killing me with these puns, Braverman."

She made an exaggerated bow. "Turtle puns are my specialty."

"Of course they are. Now, open my card."

Abby slipped her finger under the flap of the red envelope. She pulled out the store-bought card and read it to herself.

"Out loud."

"Okay. First, that's a cute cat on the front."

"Thought you'd like it."

Abby wasn't really a cat person. She liked turtles, dogs, owls, and penguins, but she didn't tell Conrad that because she didn't want to hurt his feelings. Abby cleared her throat, opened the card, and read what was inside. "On Valentine's Day, I hope you know I think you're purr-fect." It was signed: *Your friend, Conrad.*

Abby had signed hers: *Yours turtle-y, Abby and Fudge*

Conrad looked so hopeful that Abby wanted to make sure she let him know how much she appreciated it. He'd probably spent a long time at the store picking it out.

Abby closed Conrad's card and held it to her heart. "It's paws-itively fur-fect."

"Braverman!"

"Isn't it PUN-derful?" Abby laughed.

"Stop!" Conrad groaned.

Abby couldn't believe how bubbly she felt today, like the glass of champagne her moms had allowed her to have on New Year's Eve. A tiny twist of guilt poked at Abby's gut because the joy she felt today was in such sharp contrast to how dejected Paul seemed. She wished Paul could feel as happy as she did right now. After all he'd been through, he deserved to be happy more than she did.

Mama Dee came out of the bedroom. "Okay, let's get you two on your way."

Yes, let's! Abby thought. She wanted to reach out and hold Conrad's hand, but she didn't dare.

Mama Dee parked in the gravel lot at Winding River Park, startling a peacock who was strutting nearby. "I'll be back here at three o'clock to pick you up. Make sure you're right here waiting for me. If you need me before then, call or text."

"Thanks, Mama Dee." Abby kissed her on the cheek.

"Yeah, thanks," Conrad said from the back seat.

"And don't get eaten by an alligator!"

"Not on our list of things to do today," Abby assured her.

"Well, that's good to know," Mama Dee said.

Abby and Conrad got out of the car and were almost at the entrance before Mama Dee drove off.

Sunlight sparkled through the canopy of trees. Abby couldn't believe how magical it felt walking over the bridge to enter the park with Conrad.

Before they got to the last plank of the bridge, she felt him slip his warm hand into hers, intertwining their fingers.

Her breath caught. He must have had the same idea she did earlier. Abby squeezed his fingers once gently and made a mental note that this would be the first thing she'd tell Cat about the next time they video chatted.

Abby and Conrad walked like that, hand in hand, to the trailer by the bank of the river that rented kayaks and canoes.

"What're we doing?" Abby let go of Conrad's hand.

He smiled. "I reserved kayaks for—"

"You what?"

"Two single kayaks."

"That wasn't in our plan, Conrad Miller."

"I know." He smirked. "Sometimes, plans are better with a surprise tucked inside them. Don't worry. They have life jackets."

"I'm not worried. I've kayaked here with my family before."

"Oh, cool. I haven't. Mom's not into that stuff."

"Then maybe you should be the one who's worried."

"Maybe I should . . . but I'm not. Because I'm with you."

Even though it was cool outside, Abby's cheeks heated up from his words.

Conrad paid, and they got their life jackets on and their kayaks into the water.

"I hope we don't fall out," Conrad said. "It's too cold."

"We'll be good," Abby said, enjoying being the one who had more experience kayaking. "Just don't lean over too far."

"Believe me," Conrad said. "I won't."

Abby thought he looked a little unsure, but after some paddling, he seemed more comfortable.

They saw a small gator on the riverbank. And Abby pointed to a half dozen turtles sunning on a log. They splashed into the water one by one as Abby and Conrad paddled past.

Before long, they came to the part of the river that made Abby nervous. It was a mini waterfall. Brave people rode their kayaks over it with a big splash at the bottom. Abby had pulled her kayak off to the side the last time they were there and watched the people who went over the falls. She wanted to be among them, but she was afraid. Mama Dee had ridden over it with a loud *Wahoo!* when she'd splashed down at the bottom. Paul had splashed down the falls too. *Come on, Abs. It's fun!* Paul had called.

But Mom Rachel and Abby had dragged their kayaks down the ramp built beside the mini waterfall—the ramp built for cowards.

"Do we get out here?" Conrad asked before the falls. "That looks like a scary drop."

Abby stared down beyond the small falls.

Being brave is when you're scared to do something but you choose to do it anyway because you know it's the right thing to do. Abby was determined to be Abby 2.0—the best, bravest version of herself.

Without answering, she paddled straight ahead. Suddenly, the front of the kayak dropped down, and Abby was sure she'd made a terrible mistake, but it was too late to change her mind. She held her breath, prepared to be dumped into the cold, churning water and maybe even hit her head on a rock. Instead, the kayak plunged downward with a quick whoosh. Then it hit the water with a thump and a splash. She'd done it! Abby held her oar up in triumph. "Yes!"

She looked back.

Conrad was dragging his kayak down the ramp. "You're brave, Braverman!" he shouted. "Livin' up to your name."

His words and what she'd just done made her feel fantastic.

After returning their kayaks, Abby and Conrad headed to the picnic pavilion.

Conrad held her hand again, so it was hard for Abby to focus on anything, like looking out for baby owls or spotting grazing deer. The sensations coming from their intertwined fingers sent electric sparks through her whole body.

As they walked past tall pine trees on the way to the picnic pavilion and a cool breeze blew past them, Conrad said, "Whose woods these are, I think I know."

Abby stopped.

When she looked at Conrad, he was grinning.

He pulled her hand. "Come on."

They kept walking.

Abby said, "His house is in the village, though."

Conrad continued, "He will not see me stopping here."

They said the next line of Robert Frost's "Stopping by Woods on a Snowy Evening" poem together: "To watch his woods fill up with snow."

Abby tried to imagine these woods filling up with snow but couldn't because it never got cold enough to snow where they lived in South Florida.

The two of them finished reciting the poem, saying the lines together at the same time.

"How did you . . . ?" Abby asked.

"My dad. Told you he loved poetry. We memorized that one when I was younger. It stuck with me."

"That's one of the first poems I ever memorized," Abby said.

He gently swung their arms as they continued walking.

Abby was too excited to eat much of the picnic they'd put in their backpacks. She finished half a sandwich and nibbled on one cookie.

They sat on top of a picnic table to eat.

Sun shone through the trees.

The river hurried along beside them, ripples glistening.

"This is perfect," Abby said.

Conrad wiped his mouth with the back of his hand. "Not perfect. It needs one more thing to make it perfect."

Abby couldn't imagine what that could be because it was a spectacular day already, especially with her and Conrad having memorized the same Robert Frost poem when they were younger and reciting it together in the woods. She wiped a cookie crumb off the corner of her mouth. "What's that?"

Conrad looked into Abby's eyes. "Can I kiss you?"

Abby's heart responded to his words before she'd even fully heard them. Then she nodded.

He leaned forward and pressed his soft lips against hers.

When they separated, Abby blinked.

"There," Conrad said. "Now, it's a perfect Valentine's Day date."

Abby felt like she'd explode with joy. She wondered if he was going to kiss her again.

Conrad checked his phone. "Abby?"

"Mm-hmm?" She felt like she was floating on fluffy clouds of happiness.

"How far are we from the entrance?"

"I think we're about a twenty-minute walk away. Why?"

He tapped his phone. "Uh, it's ten minutes before three."

Abby's eyes went wide. *How had the time passed so quickly?*

They shoved everything into their backpacks and ran, laughing all the way out of the park. Before they got to the bridge, Abby spied a big pine cone and stopped to scoop it up and shove it into her backpack.

Then their feet clomped over the wooden bridge, and they reached the parking lot just as Mama Dee pulled up. Panting, they bent forward to catch their breaths, then high-fived each other.

"How was it?" Mama Dee asked as they got into the car.

"Perfect," they said at exactly the same time.

Later that evening, Abby wrapped the pine cone in a box with tissue paper and a ribbon. She made a card to go with it and left it on the counter in the bathroom she shared with Paul.

> *Something from Winding River Park until we can go on one of our never-ending hikes there again. Happy Valentine's Day to the World's Best Brother!*
> *Love you, Paul!*

The next morning, Abby found a single Turtles candy— pecans and caramel dipped in chocolate—on the counter next to a purple Post-it note.

> *Love you, Six-pack!*

The Unexpected

U sually, Abby woke up happy the morning of Passover
dinner because she knew she'd see her extended family.
But this Passover meant something else—something
that didn't make Abby the least bit glad. Conrad was going to
the airport to fly to his dad's house and spend nine whole days
away over spring break.

Since Conrad's mom had to work today, Abby begged
her moms to take him to the airport. She wanted all the
time she could get with Conrad before he left, but she knew
her moms would be busy preparing for Passover and would
probably say no. Abby was surprised by their unexpected
response. They agreed right away.

Abby wore her favorite purple top, her nice jeans, and her
Converse sneakers.

In the kitchen, Abby bobbed from foot to foot. She
didn't have an appetite for breakfast. She was too sad about
Conrad leaving.

"Lemme just grab a coffee to go," Mama Dee said.

Then she looked over at Mom Rachel, and they winked at each other, which Abby thought was strange.

Mom Rachel got her purse. "I'm sooooooo glad I did most of the holiday cooking yesterday. We're not going to feel like cooking much when we get back."

"I'm not going to feel like doing anything," Abby said, expecting to feel absolutely miserable after Conrad left.

Mama Dee pulled her into a hug and patted her hard on the back. "It'll be okay. It's only nine days."

"But—"

"Seriously, Abs," Mom Rachel said. "Trust us on this. You'll be fine."

"Absolutely fine." Mama Dee seemed too happy.

"You're both acting weird," Abby said.

Mama Dee took a swig of her coffee. "Oh, Abby, we're not acting."

Both her moms cracked up, like it was the funniest thing anyone ever said.

Abby shook her head and gave Miss Lucy a treat. "At least you're not acting weird," she said to the dog. The truth was, it was nice to see her moms filled with joy, even if it didn't match how she was feeling inside. There'd been so many unhappy days with Paul's surgery and treatments that Abby wasn't going to complain about her moms acting extra happy.

Miss Lucy peed on the kitchen floor at the same time that the doorbell rang.

"I've got this mess," Mom Rachel said. "You get the door."

"Thanks, Mom."

When Abby swung the door open, Conrad stood there with his suitcase. He wore a button-down shirt, jeans, and sneakers.

"Guess you're really leaving," Abby said.

"Guess so." Conrad looked both ways, then gave Abby a quick kiss. "Had to sneak one in before we're with your moms."

Abby's cheeks exploded with heat.

"Why, my lady, me doth think you're blushing."

Abby pulled Conrad inside the house. "You've been reading too much Shakespeare in your language arts class."

"Fiddlesticks, you might be right, my lady." He made an exaggerated bow.

"Fiddlesticks? My lady?" Abby shook her head. "Everyone is acting so weird."

Miss Lucy charged into the living room, sniffed Conrad's sneakers, and rolled over to give him her belly to pet.

"Gonna miss you, girl," he said.

Abby knew he was talking to the dog, but his words went straight to her heart.

I'm going to miss you too, Conrad.

The closer they got to the airport, the sadder Abby felt.

By the time they arrived to drop Conrad off at his terminal, she had to bite her bottom lip to keep from crying. She didn't want Conrad to remember her with a blotchy red face and her eyes and nose all leaky, so she'd hold it together, at least until he was inside the airport.

Mama Dee helped get Conrad's suitcase out of the trunk. "You sure you'll be okay in the airport by yourself?" she asked.

Conrad nodded. "Yeah, I've done this before. I'll be okay, but I'll call if I have a problem."

"Sounds good."

Mom Rachel jumped out of the car to give Conrad a quick hug. "Take care, sweetie. Have fun with your dad."

Conrad nodded. "Thanks for the ride."

Abby gave Conrad a hug, memorizing how solid he felt, and watched him walk into the airport. Back in the car, she slumped down in the back seat.

"Hey," Mama Dee said from the front passenger seat. "Let's go out for a quick bite at Harold's."

Harold's was an old diner her moms loved near the airport.

"Not in the mood," Abby said, looking into the airport, irritated at how happy her moms still sounded.

"It'll cheer you up," Mom Rachel said. "Besides, I'm hungry."

"Oh, me too," Mama Dee said, patting her belly. "One cup of coffee isn't gonna fill this."

Mom Rachel laughed as she pulled away from the curb.

Abby said nothing. As her mom drove away from the airport, she knew she would be too sad to eat a thing.

0 0 0

After lunch, where Abby ate a total of one french fry from Mama Dee's plate, Mom Rachel drove them back to the airport.

"What are you doing?" Abby asked. A tiny spark of hope flickered inside her. Had something happened to Conrad's flight? Were they picking him up to take him home? "Did Conrad text you about his flight being canceled or something?"

The moms didn't answer her.

Mama Dee was furiously texting.

"What's going on?" Abby asked, peering out the car's window. "Seriously, why won't either of you answer me?" Abby felt invisible. "Why are we at the airport again?"

She looked through the glass walls at the airport, hoping to get a glimpse of Conrad, even though she knew deep in her heart he was probably already on the plane that would take him to his dad's house. But why else would her moms go back to the airport? Something must have happened to his flight. Maybe it was postponed until tomorrow and she'd get one more day with him.

Mama Dee made a strange noise, like a laugh bubbling up, so Abby turned to look at the back of her moms' heads.

Mom Rachel turned to Abby with a huge grin on her face.

Abby looked toward the airport again, and out of the airport doors came someone carrying a red suitcase and looking around.

Abby blinked a few times, then exploded from the car.

She tackled her best friend in a hug. "Cat!"

Cat had dropped her suitcase and held on to Abby in a death grip. The two swayed back and forth.

When they broke apart, both girls had tears streaming down their cheeks.

"How? When?" It was all Abby could get out.

"We planned it . . . to surprise . . ." Cat couldn't catch her breath. "You!"

They hugged again.

Cat's hair smelled like strawberries.

"I can't believe . . ." Abby swiped tears from her cheeks. "You're here! You're actually here!"

"I'm here!"

They held hands and jumped up and down together.

When Abby turned, both her moms were standing at the curb, heads tilted toward each other.

"Bring it on in," Mama Dee said, opening her arms to Cat.

Cat ran to Mama Dee.

They all ended up in a four-person hug, and Abby couldn't have been happier.

After the moms put Cat's suitcase in the car, they gave each other a high five. "Nailed it," Mama Dee said.

"Not easy to keep a big surprise like that from a smarty-pants like you." Mom Rachel tousled Abby's hair.

Abby and Cat sat in the back seat together.

"I can't believe you're here," Abby said.

"I can't believe I'm here," Cat said. "Your face is thinner." Cat touched Abby's cheek.

"Your hair is lighter."

"You seem taller," Cat commented.

"You do too," Abby said.

The whole way home, they tripped over their words catching up on everything, until Cat got quiet as they drove down their street.

"Everything looks the same, but also different."

"Going away changes your perspective," Mom Rachel said.

Cat grabbed Abby's hand and squeezed. "It changes everything."

"Except our friendship," Abby whispered.

Cat nodded. "Except that."

As soon as they parked, Cat hurried out of the car. "It's weird pulling into your driveway instead of ours. And even weirder that a new family lives in our house now."

Abby thought of Conrad. She realized it was the first time she had since Cat arrived.

"Cat!" Paul ran out of the house and grabbed her into a bear hug on the front lawn.

"Paul! Miss Lucy!"

Cat scooped up Miss Lucy, who miraculously did not pee on her. But she did lick her face nonstop until she put her back down.

"You did lose weight," Cat said to Paul.

Abby put her arm around Paul's waist and squeezed. "Actually, he's gained a bunch back already. Right, Paul?"

"Hard not to gain weight when both your moms are chefs."

"I know." Cat jumped up and down. "I'm so excited. I can't wait to eat all their good food. I love the food in Israel, but I've missed your moms' cooking and baking so much."

Mom Rachel kissed Cat on top of her head. "We've missed you and your mom." She pressed her hands to her heart. "So much!"

"Yes!" Mama Dee grabbed Cat's suitcase and brought it inside.

By the time Abby, Cat, Paul, and Miss Lucy went in, the moms were in the kitchen, laughing and getting Passover dinner together for when everyone arrived later that afternoon.

Paul, Cat, and Abby sat on the back patio, talking.

Mom Rachel brought out limeade spritzers with mint leaves on top.

Cat touched Paul's hair. "It's soft."

"Yeah, it's growing back different, but the moms think it'll get back to the way it was soon."

"Paul?" Cat said in a serious tone.

"Yeah?"

"I'm so glad you're going to be okay."

He laughed. "You and me both. This was really hard. The moms took me to a therapist a couple times, and that helped. I'm just glad I'm finally feeling better, more like myself."

Those words made Abby's heart happy. She hadn't known about the therapist, but she was glad Paul had someone to talk to who could give him extra help.

"You still playing the banjo?" Cat asked.

"Yeah. Wanna hear a new song I came up with?"

"Yes!" Both girls answered at once.

Paul brought his banjo out and played an upbeat tune using his three steel finger picks.

The notes floated into Abby's ears and found their way deep into her heart. She wrapped her arms around her knees, soaking it all in—the music, Cat's surprise visit, and Paul acting like his old self.

When the extended family arrived, everyone made a big fuss about Cat being there.

"Our other granddaughter is here!" Zeyde Jordan announced.

Bubbe Marcia hugged Cat, then gave Paul a big squeeze. "I'm so glad you're doing better, *bubbelah*."

"Me too," Paul said.

"And look at that hair!" Bubbe patted the hair on Paul's head. "It's coming in curly."

Paul touched his hair. "It's like I got a perm. I'm pretty sure it will straighten out and get back to normal soon."

Zeyde Jordan cleared his throat. "Did you all hear the one about—"

"No!!!" Mom Rachel moaned, and everyone laughed.

Zeyde reached into his pocket and pulled out three twenties—one for Abby, one for Paul, and one for Cat. "I was just going to say, why is money called 'dough'? Because we all knead it." He paused. "Get it? Knead, as in—"

"They get it, Jordan!" Bubbe Marcia shook her head.

Everything was exactly like it was supposed to be.

Despite all the boring matzo they had to eat, Abby thought it was the best holiday dinner ever.

During Cat's visit, she and Abby filled their days with all of their favorite things.

They cooked and baked together. They walked into town and visited Once Upon a Bookstore, Dee's Delights, and Perk Up.

At Perk Up, Abby ordered hot chocolate, like usual.

But Cat asked for a coffee. Black.

"When'd you start drinking coffee?" Abby asked.

Cat shrugged. "The people my age drink coffee over there."

"Oh."

"I don't really like it that much, but I guess I got used to it."

Abby thought she might try a cup of coffee next time Mama Dee was making one, but she knew she'd put in agave nectar to sweeten it and add coconut milk.

The door to Perk Up opened, and Miranda and Laura walked in.

"Cat?!" Miranda shrieked and ran over.

Cat hugged Miranda and Laura, while Abby stayed seated.

"It's so good to see you," Miranda said.

"Tell us all about Israel," Laura said.

Then Abby said something that surprised herself. "Pull up chairs and sit with us."

Miranda and Laura looked shocked, but they pulled chairs over. "Thanks, Abby," Miranda said.

"Yeah, thanks," Laura echoed.

"No problem."

"Okay." Cat leaned forward. "Fill me in on everything that's happened since I've been gone."

By the time they left, Abby felt really proud of herself. She didn't care about the boring things Miranda and Laura talked about—what happened at the mall and which boy liked each of them—but she found a way to contribute to the conversation and ask questions, especially when they asked Cat about Israel, because she couldn't get enough details about what Cat's new life was like over there.

The whole time, Abby didn't shrink into herself. She was definitely changing—becoming more comfortable with poking her head out of her shell.

Before bed that night, Abby and Cat stayed up late talking, with only the soft glow from Fudge's heat lamp illuminating the bedroom.

"Do you think you and your mom will ever come back to live here?" Abby asked.

"My mom said she thinks we'll come back in three years, when our visa expires."

Abby's stomach flipped with happiness, but then it twisted with worry. She wondered where Conrad and his mom would live when Cat and her mom returned to their house. "Where will you live?" Abby asked.

Cat shrugged. "In our house next door, I guess."

"Yeah, of course," Abby said. She decided not to think about it because that was a long way off. Abby knew it would be great to have both Cat and Conrad living nearby, if that could work out.

The last night Cat was with them, the moms made a feast, including vegetarian loaded tater tots, because they knew how much Cat loved them.

Ethan came over too. He hadn't been over in a while, so it was great to see him.

Paul played his banjo for everyone after dinner, before Mama Dee served three different desserts. "A pie course. A cake course. And a cookie course," Mama Dee said, laughing. "The perfect end to a perfect meal."

It was perfect.

Good-bye and Hello

This time, when Cat went back to the airport, Abby was sad, of course, but it wasn't an overwhelming sadness like when Cat first left. Since that summer day, Abby learned she was stronger than she'd thought and could get through hard things.

"My mom said we'll be visiting for the last two weeks of July." Cat hugged Abby on the sidewalk outside of the airport. "She already bought the plane tickets and everything."

"That's only a few months away." Abby sniffed. She couldn't believe how quickly the time with Cat had passed. "My moms will be so happy. They've really missed your mom."

"She misses them too. But she really likes her new job at the university."

Abby nodded. "I'm glad." She looked at Cat. "I'll miss you so much, but we can do this." It helped to know that Cat would be visiting again and that they'd probably be coming back for good at some point.

"We've totally got this," Cat said. "I'll text you every day."

"We'll video chat, too," Abby said.

They hugged, and when they separated, Abby realized neither of them was crying. A huge improvement over when Cat first left.

"See you this summer, Abs." Cat grabbed her suitcase and backed toward the airport.

"Can't wait!" Abby called. "We're going to have the best time!"

"The best!" Cat pumped her fist.

Abby felt her moms' hands on her shoulders.

"She'll be back soon." Mom Rachel kissed Abby on the head.

"Love that girl," Mama Dee said.

"Me too," whispered Abby.

After Cat went inside the airport, Abby and her moms drove home without saying much.

Abby guessed they might be thinking about the same thing she was—all the things that had happened from the time Cat and her mom left until now, mostly about what Paul went through with surgery and treatments. What they all endured to help him through it. And how hard it was even after he was done with the treatments.

Back home, Abby cleaned out Fudge's tank, then wrote a poem while she waited for Conrad to return later that day. She was sorry Cat didn't get a chance to meet Conrad during her visit, but she couldn't wait to talk to him about Cat's visit and find out how everything went at his dad's house. Abby wondered if Conrad had memorized any new poems while he was there.

She focused on her own poem, and the marks she was making on the page looked like musical notes, gently floating together to create a quiet rhythm.

Good-bye and Hello

Good-bye.
Good-byes are hard,
But they're followed by hellos.
Good-byes are endings,
But hellos are new beginnings.
After the good-bye,
You need to keep your eyes
And your heart open
For the next hello.
Hello.

That evening, Conrad came over as soon as he got home from the airport.

Abby opened the door before he knocked the second time. "Hey!" She loved how Conrad's face lit up as soon as he saw her.

"Hey, Abs. You look . . . happy."

She nodded. "I am."

Conrad walked in and sat on the couch with her.

Miss Lucy jumped up between them and put her head in Conrad's lap.

"Aw, missed you." He pet Miss Lucy's soft ears. "You're a good girl." Then he looked at Abby. "I missed you, Braverman."

Abby relaxed into the couch. "Missed you too. How was everything at your dad's house?"

"It was really nice. We went to the library twice, a new bookstore, and three different museums."

"Wow!"

"Yeah, they live in a big city with a lot of cool stuff. And my half brother and half sister were kind of adorable. I played basketball with them. They were almost as bad as you, Abs."

"Hey!"

Conrad held up his hands as though she might hit him, but of course she wouldn't.

"So, when will you visit them again?"

"Dad said I could spend the summer there if I wanted."

Abby's breath caught. "Will you?"

Conrad grinned. "Not sure I could be away from you that long."

Abby felt her cheeks heat up. "Yeah, that would be hard, but you should be with your dad, if you want to."

"Thanks, Abs. You're a good friend."

Abby thought that Conrad was a terrific friend too, because he was happy for her when things were going well and he was there for her when things were hard. Abby knew she didn't have a lot of friends, like some people did, but the two she had were such great ones that it felt like enough.

Abby leaned toward Conrad and gave him a quick kiss on the lips.

He touched his fingers to his lips. "What was that for?"

She shrugged. "Felt like it."

He nodded. "Good. Keep feeling like it. Now tell me all about what happened while I was gone."

So she did.

Later that night, Paul set up the Monopoly game on the table. "Let's go, Six-Pack. You can have the dog token and be the banker."

Abby sat at the table with her brother and handed out the money. "You're going down in flames, Paul. I will have no mercy on you."

"I'd expect nothing less."

Abby sipped the limeade spritzer Mom Rachel had brought out.

Paul organized his money. "There's no way you're getting all the railroads this time. Not going to happen."

"Oh, we'll see about that." Abby glanced over at her moms.

They were on the couch, watching TV with their heads leaning on each other. They held hands and looked happy and relaxed.

Abby stopped to appreciate the moment. She knew it might seem ordinary to anyone else, but to her, it was absolutely extraordinary.

Before bed that night, Abby sat in front of Fudge's tank and watched him swim from one side to the other. She touched her fingers to the glass. "Turtles have a lot going for them," she told Fudge. "They're awesome exactly as they are."

Fudge swam to where Abby's fingers were pressed against the tank, opened his mouth, and seemed to nod in complete agreement.

Author's Note

This is one of the most difficult books I've ever written. I danced around a book about a young person dealing with cancer for many years, trying to write other versions that didn't work. Maybe I wasn't ready to face painful memories yet. After I finally wrote this book, dear reader, I set it aside and completely rewrote it because I wanted an honest story that told the truth about a very challenging experience.

While the characters are creations of my imagination, the heart of the story is actually mine.

In my mid-thirties, with sons who were in second and fourth grades, I was diagnosed with ovarian cancer. That diagnosis shattered my world. I wanted to be around to help my children through the difficult things in their lives and to celebrate their joys. I wanted to celebrate the next wedding anniversary with my wonderful husband. I wanted more sunrises and sunsets. I had books to write. And, reader, I was terrified of the serious surgery and intense treatments that lay ahead for me. I remember desperately wishing I could have all of it behind me, but I knew the only way beyond it was through it. I also knew there were no guarantees I'd be okay on the other side, even though the odds were in my favor with the type of cancer I had—a dysgerminoma.

The treatments I endured were the same ones Abby's brother Paul experienced, except I had *three* weeklong rounds of chemotherapy in the hospital instead of *four*. Those with some forms of testicular cancer, like the kind bicyclist Lance Armstrong had, endure four rounds.

After having three rounds of intensive chemotherapy, I was so depleted in every way that I couldn't imagine summoning the courage to go into the hospital for a fourth round. I have great respect for those who've had to do it.

I chose to specifically feature testicular cancer in this novel because when found early, successful treatment rates are very high. People need to be comfortable using words like "testicle"—a part of the body—so that there's no shame when a young person might discover an irregularity. We want young people feeling comfortable telling parents and doctors and getting medical attention as soon as possible. The key to the best outcome is early detection. Eliminating shame or stigma can prevent suffering and save lives.

Statistics and information about testicular cancer from https://www.testicularcancersociety.org/pages/about-tc:
• Young men between the ages of fifteen and thirty-five

are at the highest risk for testicular cancer. However, it can occur in men of any age.

- One in 250 men will be diagnosed with testicular cancer at some point in their lifetime, and one in five thousand will die from testicular cancer.
- For all cases of testicular cancer, the overall five-year survival rate is 95 percent, but the key is early detection. When testicular cancer is diagnosed in early stages, meaning the cancer is confined to the testis, the five-year survival rate is 99 percent.

Common signs and symptoms of testicular cancer include:
- Painless lump or swelling of the testicle
- A change in how the testicle feels
- A dull ache in the groin or lower abdomen
- A buildup of fluid in the scrotum
- Pain or discomfort in the testicle or scrotum
- A scrotum that feels heavy or swollen
- Bigger or more tender breasts

If you notice anything unusual with your testicles, you should notify your doctor immediately. The main symptom of testicular cancer is usually a lump, hardness, or painless swelling of the testicle.

Even though we had different kinds of cancer, a lot of things that happened to Paul in the book happened to me in real life, and much more that wouldn't fit into the confines of this story. Cancer treatments are hard. Support is essential. I was fortunate to have friends and family visit me to keep my spirits up and help with daily necessities like driving my kids to school (Thanks, Deborah!) and making meals (Thanks, other Donna!). Our friends even surprised us by decorating our home for the holidays when I was hospitalized so we'd come back to a dazzling surprise; thank you, Carilynn and Don. My friend Jeanne drove 1,200 miles each way *twice* to visit me, and both my sisters made the trek to spend time with me. My friend Holly lent me a computer and kept in touch with me late into the night of my final treatment. And my writing community rallied around me with a grand "Hats Off to Donna" party—Janeen, Sylvia, Linda, Jill, Laura, Ruth, and others.

Some friends didn't show up, even some family, but there was nothing I could do about that except appreciate all the love and support I did get.

It was important for me to tell the rest of the story—what happens after surgery and treatments are over. The "after" part of the story is seldom told. I wasn't prepared for how depleted I felt after treatments ended, or how depressed I'd become. While I felt pretty terrific and was happily riding my bike for miles shortly after the surgery, the chemo treatments knocked me down as low as you could imagine. It was particularly difficult when the get-well cards, phone calls, and visits stopped and everyone went back to life as normal, but my life wasn't normal. I was exhausted, bald, and had taken an unintentional months-long break from a career I loved—writing.

After treatments end, you have to find a new normal, and that takes a while.

So, if you know anyone who's recently been through cancer treatments, check in to see how they're doing and offer to keep them company or help them if they need it. It's not easy, but love and support from friends and family make an enormous difference.

Thank you so much for allowing me to share my story—Abby's and Paul's story—with you. It's my great honor to write books that connect us to one another with shared empathy and understanding and allow us to feel less alone in the world.

We're all just walking each other home.
—Ram Dass

Acknowledgments

My husband, Dan, did such a great job taking care of me and the real world while I took care of this fictional one. Dan is my favorite part of every day.

Our sons, Jake and Andrew, continue to teach me and inspire me. I'm so grateful to be part of their lives and to love them with my whole heart.

I hit the jackpot with family, like my awesome sisters and fabulous nieces and nephews, and my dear friends, who fill my well with laughter, love, and joy.

A tip of my writerly hat to my creative cohorts, especially Jill Nadler, who wrote beside me, both literally and from 1,200 miles away, as we worked hard to reach the finish lines on our respective novels.

I'm filled with gratitude for PJ Library's generous programs that support authors who create Jewish stories. This novel is richer because of two opportunities they offered: the Author Israel Adventure trip—which allowed me to explore

Israel for eight unforgettable days—and a weeklong writing retreat in cooperation with the Yiddish Book Center.

SCBWI (Society of Children's Book Writers and Illustrators) has brought the best creative people into my life and continues to enrich my work life with meaningful connections and communities. I recommend the organization to anyone who has a passion for creating children's literature.

Please support indie bookstores (indiebound.org). They are, along with libraries, the heartbeat of a community. Our local indie bookstore, Inkwood Books, has become our second home, thanks to owner, Julie Beddingfield, and booksellers Amy, Sarah, Jen, and Basia.

A story is written in isolation, then becomes a book that makes its way into the world only with a talented publishing team behind it. I'm grateful to my incredible team at Simon & Schuster Books for Young Readers, with a special shoutout to my editor, Krista Vitola. Krista and I have worked together in different capacities since the beginning of our careers. Kendra Levin also contributed thoughtful comments and helpful suggestions to shape this story.

In memory of a remarkable person—Rachel Lozano—who, many years ago, graciously answered my questions about her cancer experience when she was a young adult. Rachel shared her talents, her compassion, and her story with the world, inspiring so many, especially her loving husband, Gabe. Read about her story here: https://afreshchapter.com/2019/05/15/from-impossible-to-probable-rachels-story/.

With deep gratitude to the wonderful nurses who cared

for me in the hospital when I was scared and vulnerable. The work you do matters more than you can imagine.

I honor my family and friends who've also battled the beast: my mom, Myrna; Cousin Shelley; Aunt Iris; Bubbe Mary; my father-in-law, Jake; my mother-in-law, Jane; my sister-in-law Janet; and friends Caren, Monica, Gail, Carole, Cary, Elysa, Maggie, Wendy, Kieran, Peter, Linda, Deborah, and Sandra.

Finally, thank you, dear reader. A story is only half-finished until it is read and a connection of shared humanity is forged.